The Mistaken Haunting of Seth Harrison

Marie LeClaire

Copyright 2022 Marie LeClaire
All rights reserved.

ISBN: 9798835782390

Cover art by Brigitte Werner courtesy of Pixabay.com

*Lizzie Borden took an axe
And gave her mother forty whacks.
When she saw what she had done,
She gave her father forty-one.*

*Andrew Borden now is dead,
Lizzie hit him on the head.
Up in heaven he will sing,
On the gallows she will swing.*

Marie LeClaire

Chapter 1

Liam could feel the knot tightening in his gut as he pulled into the parking lot of the Bridgewater State Forensic Hospital. No matter how many times he visited the prison, he couldn't shake the disconcerting feeling that came over him as soon as he passed the first gate. It was the price of being a Sensitive.

He parked his black Mercedes sedan and scanned the parking lot before getting out. He knew someone was watching him. It wasn't paranoia. It was video security.

Looking at himself in the rear-view mirror, he ran his fingers through long unruly curls, taming them as best he could. He got out of his car and immediately straightened his signature double-breasted black trench coat. It had a small cape over the shoulders like something out of the nineteenth century. He thought the look made him stand out. It did, but not in a good way.

He reached into the back seat for his black leather satchel and closed the car door. Pressing the button on his key fob elicited a *thump* and a *whoop* as the car doors locked. He turned and headed toward the prison entrance. Suddenly, he was jerked backward, twisting and slamming into his car.

Marie LeClaire

"What?! What!?" he shouted, swiveling his head from side to side, near panic. He saw no one. Looking further, he noticed his coat, held tightly in the car door.

"God damn it!" He looked around again. This time checking to see if anyone was nearby. He groped around in his pocket for his key fob, inadvertently hitting the alarm button.

The car screamed *Whoooop! Whoooooop! Whoooooop!*

"Shit!" Fumbling with the keys, he finally opened the door and silenced the alarm. He slammed the door shut, straightened his jacket and headed to the building, kicking the tire as he went by. He had regained his composure by the time he got to the security checkpoint.

"Hey, Doc," the guard greeted him as he buzzed him into the lobby. "Having a bit of car trouble?"

"Damn panic buttons," Liam growled, straightening his coat. "Officer Tindel. Nice to see you." He made it a habit to learn the names of all the guards he encountered regularly. The personal touch could go a long way if he needed something in the future. He placed his valise on the conveyor belt.

"Still working on that paper?" the guard queried.

Liam dodged questions about his work with academic babble. "Yes. It's a longitudinal study on behavior modifications based on duration of incarceration, so it's not likely to be published for another couple of years, pending review from the Forensic Psychology Board at UMass."

"Sure, whatever you say." Officer Tindel sent the bag through the x-ray machine where a second guard reviewed its contents. "Go on in."

Liam advanced through the metal detector, as the guard circled around, meeting him on the other side. "Who can we pull for you today?"

"No one special, thank you. I'm only observing the yard activities today."

"Suit yourself. Let us know if there's anything you need."

Liam retrieved his briefcase from the belt. "I certainly will." He headed down the hallway toward the next locked door.

"I'll call ahead and let them know you're coming."

"Thank you," Liam called back.

As a sociology professor at the University of Massachusetts, Dr. Liam McMurty could talk his way into any public or government facility. He simply claimed that he needed information for one paper or another and people were usually eager to help. When he met with occasional resistance, he had two tactics. He either baited them with a mention in his paper, appealing to the ego-driven, or made subtle threats of a poor report to higher-ups in the chain. So far, this strategy had gained him entry anywhere he wanted to visit.

Today he was at Bridgewater State Hospital, a facility for the criminally insane, where security was high, with two concentric razor wire fences circling the property. It was the only forensic psychiatric hospital in Massachusetts and it housed the most notorious criminals, past and present. The Boston Strangler spent some time here in the 1960s before being transferred to the federal prison in Walpole, but most inmates died here, literally fulfilling their life sentence.

He continued down the long gray hallway from the entrance.

"Good morning, Doc."

"Sergeant." Liam nodded to the officer as he passed through the locked doors separating the admin offices from the inmate area.

His destination today was the Outer Wall, a six-foot thick barrier of poured concrete that surrounded the entire facility. As he made his way through the stark corridors, the air became increasingly stale with the smell of stone and poor ventilation. He was grateful to get to the next security checkpoint at the bottom of the stairs that would bring him back out into fresh air. There was no x-ray machine here, but the arch of a metal detector did another scan.

"Good morning, sir. Empty your pockets please." The guard shoved a small dirty plastic bowl at him. "Open your briefcase. Place it on the table."

"Certainly, officer." Liam purposefully leaned down to read the officer's name tag. *Sgt. Cameron Borden.* "Are you new here, Sergeant Borden?"

"No sir."

"I don't recall seeing you here before, that's all."

"Not my usual station. I'm just covering for the day...sir." The guard barely glanced at Liam, annoyance creeping into his voice.

"Do you know who I am, sergeant?"

"Dr. McMurty, I understand, here to study the inmates for your next paper."

Liam's chest pumped out slightly at the recognition. "So, you're familiar with my work?"

"I'm aware that you haven't actually published anything in eight years."

The Mistaken Haunting of Seth Harrison

Liam's back went ramrod straight. His defenses went up. "Oh," he tried not to sneer, "A well-informed prison guard. How unusual."

"Just doing my job...sir...wondering how a civilian gets permission to walk the P." The slang was a reference to the Perimeter, a walkway on the top of the Outer Wall that overlooked The Yard, the only outdoor space available to the prisoners. Along the P stood three towers manned 24/7 with snipers.

"Well, Google doesn't know everything, sergeant."

"No, sir." The guard reviewed the contents of the bowl and briefcase while Liam passed easily through the security arch.

"All clear, sir."

"Thank you." Liam picked up his things and headed up the stairs. He didn't like this new guard. There was something off about him, aside from being an ass. The last thing he needed was an overachiever nosing around in his business. On the other hand, he had to admire the guard for doing more investigation than anyone else had done in the five years he'd been coming here. He decided the man would make a better ally than adversary and didn't pursue the argument.

Liam pushed through the door at the top of the stairs, took in a deep breath of fresh air and waited a moment for his eyes to adjust to the daylight. The guard in the corner shack a hundred yards away gave him a wave, acknowledging his arrival. Liam waved back a two-fingered salute from an imagined hat brim.

After walking about halfway to the corner, he turned his attention to the interior courtyard. Referred to simply as The Yard, it was about the size of a football field and the most volatile area of the prison. It was empty except

Marie LeClaire

for the Yard Guards, a team of six officers specifically trained for this position. An eerie silence floated over the compound as Liam waited for the doors to open and the inmates to arrive. He took the time to study the guards below. Surprising to some, they were not heavily armed, carrying only nightsticks and tasers. The real firepower was with the snipers who could pick off an inmate anywhere in the yard with deadly accuracy.

A loud siren broke the silence as doors clanged open. Inmates flooded the dirt arena. It was a sociologist's playground and any of his colleagues would be quick to point out this behavior or that, but prison social norms were the least of his interests. He was looking for the "Odd People," rare individuals with mystical or psychic traits that often got themselves into trouble, landing them in either prisons or mental hospitals or, in this case, both.

Today there were close to one hundred prisoners in the yard, some agitated, pushing and shoving other inmates, some over-medicated, shuffling along staring at the ground. The guards in the Yard and on the Wall were on high alert.

Liam had taken out a notebook and was placing hash marks in various boxes as he watched the activity in the yard.

"Seeing anything noteworthy?"

Liam jumped slightly, following it with exaggerated posturing trying to cover it up. It was Sgt. Borden from downstairs. He had made his way to Liam's side completely unnoticed.

"Ah, well, hard to say, really. Nothing I wasn't expecting. Today's visit was only to confirm my data. Research is all about the details." The sergeant remained silent. Liam's antenna was up. There was something unusual about this man. Was he an Odd Person? He didn't seem to be. Then what was it?

"How long have you been here, Sergeant Borden? My studies include the workforce too, you know. What calls a person to this kind of work and so forth."

"I've been here about two years now. Usually, I'm patrolling the grounds, inside and outside the Wall."

"Really? I wouldn't think the outside needed much security."

"It's mostly curious teenagers or homeless guys looking to camp out over by the trees."

Sgt. Borden was staring out over the wall to the back of the property. In 1855, when Bridgewater first opened as an insane asylum, its compound was over a hundred acres and included a working farm, complete with chickens, cows and sheep. Patients were expected to work as part of their treatment and the farm made the facility almost self-sufficient. Social activists of the 60s condemned it as forced labor and the practice ceased.

The property gradually transitioned into a multi-use facility with the maximum-security forensic hospital occupying the original inpatient domicile and hospital ward. The wall was added in 1969 and topped with razor wire in 1978 following an escape attempt.

"I hear it's haunted out there," Liam offered. The guards were a superstitious lot and Liam expected a reaction. The sergeant continued his long-distance stare. Was he looking at the Link? Liam couldn't tell.

"So they say," he nodded, continuing to look into the distance.

Liam took a moment to look him over. Sgt. Borden, about thirty by Liam's guess, was wearing the standard guard uniform, a black polo shirt and gray chino pants tucked into black steel-toed boots. Liam noticed a chain around his neck. Some guards wore talismans or religious charms for protection.

"I notice you're wearing a chain. Mind if I ask what's on it?"

"What's it to you?"

"Professional curiosity."

Sgt. Borden reluctantly pulled out the chain. Liam felt a slight energy wave pass through his body. His suspicions were confirmed when the sergeant revealed a Caller Coin, an eight-sided brass medallion, the size of a half-dollar, plain except for two fine lines etched around the edges on both sides with a gothic-styled design in the center. Liam struggled to feign disinterest.

"That's interesting. What is it?"

"Some old relic my grandfather gave me. Said it warded off evil spirits and stuff."

Liam read the slight increase in tension in Borden's body. He knew he was lying. "So far, so good?"

"Yeah, so far."

"Well, thank you, Sgt. Borden. I think I have all I need for today. Do you need to walk me out?"

"Just down to the security check-point. Then you can make your way to the front." He gestured toward the stairs.

"Maybe I can walk the outer grounds with you someday. Get your view on things." Liam had been looking for an excuse to go out back ever since he noticed the gray iridescent oval on the outside of the wall four years ago. He strongly suspected it was a Link, tears in the time continuum, that allowed a person to travel to another location instantly, but he needed a closer look.

"I don't see the point."

The Mistaken Haunting of Seth Harrison

"Professional curiosity. A chance to see what remains of the old farm."

"You're quite the curious guy, Dr. McMurty."

"Yes, I am, Sgt. Borden. So, what do you say?"

"You'll have to clear it with Admin."

"But you don't have any objections?"

"I guess not."

"Excellent."

When they arrived back at the checkpoint, Sgt. Borden stayed behind, studying Liam as he headed back to the entrance. As soon as Liam was out of sight, he pulled a cell phone from his pants pocket, looked around to ensure privacy and pushed a few buttons.

"You were right," he said into the phone. "I just bumped into McMurty. He's up to something, I'm sure. He asked to go walking around outback...Yeah, I'll keep you posted."

Once back to his car, Liam allowed himself a grin and a small fist pump of excitement at his amazing find. A Caller Coin! And an excuse to walk around the grounds! He looked back at the old brick building. "Well," he said into the air. "It looks like my luck keeps getting better and better."

Links were literally the stuff of legends. Whenever he heard stories of mysterious places, hauntings, or unexplained disappearances, he was quick to check them out. Bridgewater State Hospital was full of these stories and, as it turns out, for good reason. Links were rare and unnoticed by most humans. He was pretty sure Bridgewater State Hospital had one. As excited as he was about his discoveries at the prison, a more interesting prize

Marie LeClaire

lay just two buildings over at Home Away From Home Child and Adolescent Treatment Center, his second stop today.

    The Consortium had mocked his visits here as wishful thinking and unlikely to yield anything of value.
"I don't see why you continue to visit those dreary places, Liam. You'd have much more luck following up on the scandal sheets," Marilisa, the secretary of the Chairwoman admonished him. "They all think you're wasting your time."

As a result, he refrained from sharing his discoveries. Now, he stood by his car staring out over the property, bragging to himself. "One Link, one Caller Coin and Seth Harrison."

Chapter 2

Seth stared at the antiseptic white walls and the unbreakable metal furniture of the small conference room. Its plexiglass windows looked out on the common area of Ward B, his home for the past year. Across from him, Ms. Jennifer had his medical file open on the table. It was thicker than he remembered.

"So, Seth, do you have a discharge plan like we've been talking about? Like a place to live?"

"Todd told me there's a nice bridge at 11th Street and Jefferson." Seth ran a hand through his dark hair, pushing it out of his eyes, and flashing her a weak smile. His boyish charm could go a long way with Ms. Jen and he was hoping to lessen her irritation at his lack of progress.

"Seriously, living in a cardboard box under a bridge is NOT a discharge plan."

"I wasn't considering the box. Now it sounds even better." His smile was half-hearted.

"Seth," she admonished him.

"Jennifer," he played her tone back.

"You need to take this more seriously. You only have three weeks left."

Seth pushed himself back from the table. "What do you want me to say? I've got no family, no friends, a shitty part-time job, and, in three weeks, no place to live.

Marie LeClaire

"I'm not saying it's a great situation but there has to be a plan." She waved loose papers at him. "Most kids think turning eighteen is a big deal, free to do whatever they want. This is your chance to make all those decisions about your life."

"Well, most kids don't get kicked out of their house as a birthday present."

Seth Harrison had arrived on the ward a year ago after bouncing between foster families and group homes since age ten. He was fated to spend his last year of youth services here at the Bridgewater site. In three weeks, when he turned eighteen, Seth would age out of the system. Not being sick enough to warrant placement in an adult group home, he was scheduled to be discharged into the real world with the support of an overworked case manager and five hundred dollars.

"The foster care system isn't set up to keep kids after they turn eighteen. You know that. You've known that for years." She leaned over the table, almost pleading with him to put some effort into it. "So why are you making this so hard?"

Seth threw his hands up. "Well, what do you suggest?" he asked, even though he already knew the answer.

"You know what my plan is. Go full-time at Quick Lube, find an affordable apartment and the agency will help you get furniture and household goods. If you have a better plan, now's the time to speak up. Otherwise, I'm moving forward with this before we run out of time. What do you say?"

"I guess I'm hoping for that long-lost relative to show up and take me home to some big house in a nice neighborhood." Seth hung his head slightly, looking down

The Mistaken Haunting of Seth Harrison

at his hands folded on the table in front of him, his vulnerability surfacing.

"We've looked every way we can think of to find family. You know that." Jennifer was sympathetic. She'd had these conversations a hundred times before and they didn't get any easier.

"Alright, let's look for an apartment. I'll ask at work tomorrow about full time."

"Great. It's a start. And if something changes, we can revise our plan. Sign here." Jennifer slid a form across to Seth outlining the plan. He signed it with disinterest.

Jennifer attached the lose pages to the metal pegs in the chart and smoothed them flat. "Don't worry. It will all work out," she said as she left the room, anxious to get moving on the paperwork while she still had Seth's buy-in.

Liam pulled into the parking lot adjacent to the prison, outside the razor wire, where the six remaining buildings of the original State Hospital were used by various city departments. Since 1990, one of these buildings served as an inpatient psychiatric facility for children and adolescents. Liam was a regular visitor.

"Good morning, Dr. McMurty," the unit clerk flashed him a flirtatious smile. "You know the drill." She handed him a clipboard.

He took it, returning her smile. "Good morning, Delia. Has anything exciting happened since last week?" He signed in, noting the time, and handed it back to her.

"Let's see. I broke up with my boyfriend. My mother's dog finally died and my neighbor's teenage son burned down their garage trying to disassemble a hoverboard." She was leaning over the reception counter, making sure Liam had a view down her scrubs.

Marie LeClaire

"Well, that's very interesting." His eyes lingered a moment. "But I was thinking more along the lines of here at the hospital."

"Oh, right. Of course. No. Not much. Well, you know Seth's getting out in a few weeks."

"Yes. I know."

"He's not taking it well and he's giving Miss Jennifer a run for her money. I'm staying out of her way. I suggest you do the same."

"Thanks for the heads up."

"No problem."

A buzzer sounded and Liam opened the door to the secure ward.

Liam had recognized Seth as an OP, his own code for Odd Person, a year ago, immediately after he was admitted. Seth was at least a Sensitive like himself, and likely more, judging by the iridescent aura surrounding him. The boy seemed to have no idea about who or what he was. On the contrary. A benevolent but misguided youth services system had convinced Seth that he was mentally ill, which is typical for children with unusual gifts. Liam had tried to make this point to the Consortium without success. Their attitude was that special children had special parents keeping an eye out for them. It hadn't been true for Liam, and it certainly wasn't true for Seth. It was a situation Liam planned to take full advantage of, but he needed to make sure the timing was right.

Each patient signed a release to the University of Massachusetts for statistical information, so he was able to access Seth's file easily by flashing his university badge and claiming research needs. The records were relatively sparse on personal information. The diagnosis read

The Mistaken Haunting of Seth Harrison

Psychosis Not Otherwise Specified – Unremitting. In layman's terms, it meant Seth had hallucinations that couldn't be medicated away. The reason, Liam knew, was because they weren't hallucinations. Liam had seen them too. Two ghosts appeared to be stalking the boy. They were quick to vanish when other people were around though, making it appear as if Seth had a psychotic disorder. Liam did nothing to dispel the idea.

As for Seth's family, Liam's questions were answered in a short note on the first page. *Parents both dead, tortured to death by home intruders when patient was ten years of age. No other family found.* An accompanying newspaper clipping indicated that Seth had remained hidden in the garage for almost two days until the mailman noticed something funny and called the police.

Seth's life in state custody had been rocky from the start, but when the hallucinations started at age thirteen, it went from bad to worse. His first hospitalization was a year later when he was kicked out of his third foster home for seeing things that weren't there and scaring the other children. Now, four years later, Seth was aging out of the system.

Liam spotted Seth, seated alone in one of the meeting rooms off of the ward's common area. Maybe this was the moment.

"Hey, Champ." Liam called from the doorway. "What's up?"

"Planning my escape with Ms. Jennifer."

"Ah. Any good options?"

"Define good."

Marie LeClaire

"You sound discouraged." A sincere concern could be heard in Liam's voice as he sat down opposite Seth. Despite his own agenda, Liam had come to like the boy.

"It's hard to get excited about living alone in a shitty apartment in a shitty neighborhood going to a shitty job every day."

"Well, when you put it like that..."

"I'm trying to be upbeat, really, but I don't see a bright future for me, working nowhere jobs and seeing a shrink for the rest of my life. And I'm still seeing those stupid hallucinations." Seth shoulders slumped.

Liam wondered if now was the time to pitch his idea. Intuitively, he went for it.

"Well, here's something to think about. Just an idea mind you. How about if you come live with me when you've worn out your welcome here?"

"What?" The astonishment on Seth's face made Liam smile, which made Seth angry. "Are you just yanking my chain, man? That's messed up!"

"No. No. Nothing like that. It was just the look on your face... that's all. No, I assure you, I'm quite serious."

Seth looked at him for a moment. "Why would you want to do that?" He had learned to be suspicious.

"I've been thinking about it for a while. It could do us both some good. You can ease into the world and I can have some company around the house which has become deafeningly quiet of late."

"What do I have to do?" Seth knew that something too good to be true usually was.

"You have to keep working, part-time at first, and you have to pay room and board. There will be an equal division of chores and you have to clean the litter box. It's the chore I hate the most."

The Mistaken Haunting of Seth Harrison

"You have a cat?" That got Seth's interest almost more than the offer itself. Growing up in group homes and treatment centers, he had always longed for a pet.

"Yes. She's a common American Tabby, nothing special, although she doesn't act like it. I'm afraid that's partly my fault. I let her pretty much run the house."

"I don't know. Let me think about it." Seth remained suspicious.

"Sure. Take your time. I know this came out of left field for you." Liam stood. "Maybe talk it over with Ms. Jennifer."

Seth watched as Liam walked out, leaving him alone again. He slumped back in his metal chair. Had everything just changed? A miracle? Who knows? But, for the first time in a long while, he allowed himself to hope.

Liam headed for the file room, suppressing a smile. That was easier than he thought it would be, but he always overcomplicated things in his head. He knew Seth would take him up on the offer and the timing was perfect. Seth's birthday was three weeks away and the pressure was on.

Liam felt the pressure as well. He wasn't sure what Seth was, but he was sure the Consortium would be interested. So would the Legion.

Chapter 3

"Hey, Millie. I'm home," Liam called out as he dropped his keys on the table beside the door.

On the couch, a gray and white tabby reluctantly stirred from her nap, ears twitching at the noise. It was her eighth nap of the day. She liked to get ten in before the evening prowl if she could. There was still time. With a large yawn, she jumped lightly to the floor and luxuriously stretched first her front legs and then her back before she wandered into sight.

"Ah, there you are. Good. We have to talk."

"Meeeaooooorrwwww."

"Yes. About Seth."

"Merr mmreeeow."

"You knew he was coming here eventually."

"Mrrww mrrrwww."

"Can you at least try to have a better attitude about it."

"Mrrrr."

"You'll like him. You'll see. How about some dinner?" Liam groped in the cupboard for the cans of boutique cat cuisine, causing an avalanche of tiny tins to tumble out. He juggled them chaotically until they settled onto the kitchen counter.

"Here." He retrieved two options. "Seafood Scampi or Beef Bolognaise."

"Meeeoooooww."

Marie LeClaire

"Really, Millie? Do you know how much this stuff cost?"

She turned her backside to him, tail held high in the air.

"Suit yourself," he huffed, tossing the cans back into the cupboard.

With a final wave of her tail, Millie headed out the cat door to the patio and beyond, in search of something more to her liking.

Liam turned to look out at the chaos that was his house. It was an average ranch home with an open L-shaped layout affording him wide view of its contents. It wasn't dirty, exactly, but no one would accuse him of being compulsively organized.

In addition to his search for Odd People, he had become a collector of Odd Things, everyday items that had a magical glow to them indicating some supernatural quality. He found them mostly at estate sales and antique shops. Once he got them home, Millie would sniff out any value. She had a nose for it. The result was a handful of minimally magical things with the occasional jackpot item, and a house full of other stuff of no use whatsoever, at least no current use.

Mostly, they were old touchstones, items that had belonged to spirits that lingered here before making the final journey. They had a slightly amber aura with a purple halo, like his grandfather's ring. He felt fortunate to have spent time with his grandfather's spirit when he was a boy. The ring was all he had left. His father was another story.

He picked up a large file box containing some of his father's belongings and placed it on the dining table. If his father was dead, Liam hoped one of these items might be a touchstone. If he were alive, they might be clues to his

The Mistaken Haunting of Seth Harrison

whereabouts. He hesitated with his hands on the lid, then decided there was no point in going through it again. He'd find space in one of the cabinets later.

He turned his attention to the living area where every flat surface was covered with something. An old oil lantern, a large bowl of skeleton keys and a twelve-arm candelabra cohabited on the coffee table. There was a jar of marbles and an old clamp-on-your-shoe roller skate on the sideboard amidst other children's items. The buffet was entirely filled with jewelry which was by far the most popular category of Odd Things. That and weaponry, mostly swords and knives, large and small, which took up the armoire beside the buffet. The adjacent cabinet contained pieces of armor, a couple of old rifles, and military bric-a-brac that had outlasted the uniforms they were once attached to. One interesting old touchstone, a long slender blade designed to be concealed in a lady's glove, stuck out of the dirt in a barely surviving aloe plant.

Not everything was a touchstone. One might have an unusual scroll or monogram. Another a faint hue of color surrounding it or a slight vibration when touched. He suspected that they once belonged to magical people. Mildred could pick out the big stuff but she didn't catch everything, like that dagger that kept disappearing. She totally missed that. He hadn't been able to grab it again since he brought it home.

"Shhhhheesshhhhh. What am I going to do with all this stuff?" He ran his fingers through his hair as he walked around the living room. He was starting to wonder if Seth would even agree to stay here. It wasn't exactly living large, or even normal. *Oh, well, normal was overrated. Anyway, Seth wasn't so normal himself.* "He has to like it here," he said out loud in response to his own

Marie LeClaire

musings. "Maybe a refrigerator stocked with frozen pizza and beer will forgive a lot of sins." Then he realized Seth wasn't old enough to drink.

He opened one of the doors in the living room armoire, which also had an orange glow, and began tossing things in.

He was fondling a small brass orb when his phone rang. He jumped in surprise. His phone hardly ever rang. He pulled it out and viewed the incoming number. It was an extension from the Bridgewater State Hospital. He had a moment of panic. Had something happened to Seth?

Liam swiped it open. "Hello?"

"Hello, Liam?"

"Yes?"

"It's Jennifer Davis, from Bridgewater State Hospital."

"Yes, Jennifer. I recognize your voice. How are you?" He tried for a casual professional tone.

"Well, I'm either very grateful or really peeved, depending on how this conversation goes."

"Ah, I'm assuming you've talked to Seth." He walked around the living room, nervously tossing things out of sight, as if she could see the state of his house.

"Yes. I have. And if this is some kind of scam, I'll have you banned from this facility forever. Am I clear?" She paused but not long enough for a response. "Did you offer to take Seth into your home?"

"Yes. In hindsight, I'm realizing just this minute, that I probably should have talked with you first, though."

"It would have been nice." Her response was icy.

"Yes. Sorry about that. It was somewhat spur of the moment, although I've had it in the back of my mind for a few months now, knowing that Seth will be heading out on his own. I was waiting to see if anything turned up for him

The Mistaken Haunting of Seth Harrison

before I said anything." With a loafered foot he slid an ornately carved wooden chess board along the carpet and under the overstuffed chair.

"So, spur of the moment you offer a desperate kid a place to stay?"

"Well, when you put it like that, it sounds a little reckless, but yes and I mean it wholeheartedly. I assure you this is not some whim that I haven't thought through." He looked around the house wondering if he really had thought it through. Just then, the dagger appeared across the room. He darted for it.

"Really? Because that's what it sounds like." The ice in her voice was not melting one bit.

"I understand your skepticism." The dagger vanished within inches of his outstretched hand. "How can I ease your concerns?" He desperately wanted to smooth this over.

"For starters you can come in tomorrow for a meeting about how you imagine this is all going to work."

"Absolutely. What time?" The dagger reappeared across the dining room table. He reached for it and missed with a huff of breath at the exertion as it disappeared again.

"What are you doing? Are you listening to me? This is important."

"Yes. Yes." Liam straightened up. "You have my full attention."

"Be in my office first thing in the morning because if you're serious, there are a lot of things that need to fall into place in three weeks."

"I am absolutely serious. I can be there at 8:30." Holding the phone between his cheek and shoulder, he used one arm to sweep a pile of nuts and bolts into an old cookie tin.

"What was that?" Jennifer demanded.

"Nothing. Nothing. Just, ah, cleaning up a bit."

"Really? It sounded like gunshots." Her tone was accusatory.

"No. No. Marbles. I'm a bit of a collector."

There was a long pause while she considered the plausibility of this.

"Fine. I'll talk more with you in the morning. And please don't have any further conversation with Seth about this until we've had a chance to talk."

"Certainly. I only see him when I'm at the hospital anyway."

"Tomorrow at 8:30. Be here." She hung up before he could respond.

Jennifer was clearly not convinced of his sincerity. For a moment, he worried that he had blown it by not talking to her first. He'd have to do some repair work tomorrow.

***

Liam walked into Jennifer's office at 8:30 sharp. She was on the phone barking orders at some poor staff member who had apparently irritated her already today. Liam braced himself as she hung up the phone.

"Sit down, please, Liam." Her words were polite. Her tone was not.

Liam decided not to challenge her authority with his usual *I'm a professor at UMass* card. "Let me start by saying again that I recognize that I might have skipped a few steps when I talked with Seth yesterday." It wasn't really an apology and they both knew it.

"I appreciate your desire to help, Liam, but this is a very serious situation and I have to be absolutely sure this is what is best for Seth."

"I understand."

"I don't think you do. First of all, you are on staff here and that raises ethical issues."

"Jennifer, I am not on staff here and you know it. I am a researcher who comes by on occasion to review files for that purpose. I have had no direct or indirect dealings with this center or with Seth's treatment. He and I have just spoken casually and have developed a friendship of sorts."

"Well, at best it's a gray area," she insisted.

"There's nothing gray about it. I'm happy to have a review board consider it but that will take weeks, and we both know, you – and Seth – don't have that kind of time."

"*And* you don't know anything about his illness." Jennifer was trying to regain the high ground. "He has unremitting psychosis. Do you even know what that means?"

"I know very well what that means."

"That means," she continued despite his response, "that he continues to hallucinate despite all pharmaceutical and therapeutic interventions. Are you willing to deal with that? It can be very disruptive. And you live alone. What is this going to do to your daily routine? It's more than just having a roommate. Do you even have a houseplant?"

"I have several plants and a cat that I've managed to keep alive for six years and counting." Liam was beginning to feel insulted.

Jennifer finally took a breath.

"Yes, of course," she backed off slightly. "I'm a little protective of my seventeen-year-olds. It's such a scary time for them. I want everything to go as smoothly as possible."

"I understand, Jennifer, and if at the end of our conversation, you think this is not in Seth's best interest, I will withdraw my offer."

Jennifer paused to consider this.

"Okay, then. Let's get to it."

Chapter 4

It was Seth's last day on the ward and once again he was sitting in the sterile meeting room with Ms. Jennifer. This time she had a box sitting on the table beside her. It was a standard file box, like he'd seen many times over the years. She looked serious which made Seth very nervous.

"Don't tell me. It all went to shit, right? No Liam. No place to live. Back to square one."

"No. No. Nothing like that. Don't even say it." Jennifer waved her hands as if she were erasing it out of the air. "Your plans are all fine. Finished. Approved."

"Then what's up? You're scaring me."

"Well, I came across something interesting when I was gathering all your files together. It has to do with your parents' death."

Seth let out a huff. "Really? Do you know how many times I've talked about this?"

"It's not like that," she countered quickly. "I found something in the original folder, from when social services picked you up at the police station." She paused to let it sink in. "It was a claim ticket from the police department personal property office."

After another long moment Seth nodded. "And?"

"With a letter indicating that they had some possessions that you were found with when the police arrived at your house that day."

Marie LeClaire

Seth took in a long breath. Was there something in there that was going to blow his plans with Liam out of the water? A reference to that long lost relative? What?

"*And?*" Seth asked again, frustration mounting.

"The letter and the ticket apparently got lost in the shuffle of those early days and... anyway, I called to see if your things were still there and they were, so I took the liberty of going to pick them up."

Seth was looking at the box on the table.

"I went through it already, just to make sure there were no surprises, well, no bad ones anyway, not that these are good ones exactly, well.... you know what I mean."

"Yeah, I get it."

"There's not much here but it's yours. It includes the clothes you were wearing that day. Apparently, the police took them as evidence along with a few other things. I'll look at them with you now if you want. Or you can take them with you."

"Now's good." Seth slowly reached for the box as Jennifer pushed it to the middle of the table between them. He lifted the lid and tipped the box so he could see the contents. Inside were several clear plastic evidence bags, taped shut, with an index card labeling the contents. On top was a small pair of tennis shoes.

He reached in and removed the bag, placing it on the table. "My mom bought me these." The next bag had a shirt and pants, still dirty from being worn that day. A memory slid into his brain of playing in the yard with his friends, building forts out of dead branches. He winced.

"Are you okay, Seth?"

"Sort of, I guess, yeah. It's just, you know, making me remember things. Just little things, like playing with friends."

The Mistaken Haunting of Seth Harrison

"You don't have to do this all at once, you know."

"No. I'm good." He reached into the box for the next bag. It contained his mother's scarf. He held it on the table in front of him, staring at it, barely breathing.

"Do you remember it, Seth? The file said you refused to let go of it. You said your mother told you never to let anyone take it from you."

Seth's face scrunched up, brows furrowed, as if trying very hard to remember something.

"I remember, just before she shoved me in the cupboard in the garage. She told me not to move a muscle, not make one sound, until she came for me. I think there was something in it." He pressed the bag in his hands, feeling around, but found nothing.

Jennifer gently took the bag from his hands. "Maybe this?" She tipped the box toward him. There was a small bag on the bottom with a single item in it.

He reached in and held it up, turning it around in the sunlight coming through the dayroom windows. It was a quartz crystal pendant on a black silk cord.

He turned it over in his hands. "She kept repeating that I shouldn't give it to anyone and did I understand. I didn't remember till just now. That was the last time I saw her."

After staring at it for a long moment, he peeled off the red tape and removed the stone. He held it in his open palm, inspecting it. It was three inches long with nearly perfect sides. Its heavier weight was the only thing that gave it away as stone and not the inexpensive glass crystals kids were wearing. It had a smoky gray tint with the top encircled by a brass band adorned with six small jewels, one topping off each facet. A black silk cord looped through the finding.

Marie LeClaire

"It's beautiful. Did she wear it much?"

"I've never seen it before. I remember that she wore a small gold charm made of three triangles overlapping each other. She said it meant the three of us."

"Well, it's yours now. Something to take with you as you head out on your own."

"Yeah. I guess. Thanks, Ms. Jennifer." He got up and put everything back in the box.

"Can I take this?" he asked, indicating the box and its contents.

"Yes. Take it all. It's yours. Let me know if you need anything."

"Yeah."

Chapter 5

When they pulled into the driveway, Seth let out a breath. It was nicer than he expected. Considering Liam's unusual appearance, the house seemed ordinary. It was a single story with a small yard that looked well cared for.

"Here we are," Liam announced as he shut off the car engine.

They walked silently to the front door, Liam leading the way.

He unlocked the door and stepped into the small entryway, waving Seth in. "Welcome home," he said nervously.

Seth stood in the doorway, holding his breath again, all hope for ordinary was gone as he looked around the inside. There was clutter everywhere, and not just the usual stuff. Old rusty things, dusty books, old photos.

Liam led him around the clutter. "This is your room, Seth." He tried for cheery.

"Yeah, thanks." Seth put his two duffel bags on the bed. He hadn't had his own room in years, not like this, anyway. He had been alone in his two-person room at the Center for some of his time there, but in the end, it was still a hospital room. He lost the only room he ever had when he was ten.

"I thought we'd get pizza tonight and talk about how exactly we're going to do this. I've lived alone for a while now and I'm used to doing things my way without much trouble, except maybe from Mildred."

"Mildred?"

"Mildred Catly. The resident feline. She's around somewhere. She might come out for pizza. She has a fondness for pepperoni."

"Seriously?" Seth looked around on the floor trying to spot her.

"Certainly. You'll like her. She takes a while to warm up to strangers though, so don't be offended."

"Sure." Seth turned his attention to the room. There was a tall dresser, an empty bookcase, and a small closet with empty hangers tangled on a pole beneath an empty shelf. He wondered if he had enough things to fill the space. The double bed felt like a true luxury compared to the twin single-mattress cot he'd grown accustomed to. Seth felt anxiety creeping in with the realization that he was really on his own now. No hospital, no social services. No safety net. He was officially and legally an *adult*. His breathing got faster and shallow. He could hear his heart pounding.

Liam saw the flush come over Seth's face. "I know it's a lot. Are you okay?"

"Just…ah…little overloaded."

"I'll give you some space. You can unpack if you like. I'll grab the rest of the boxes from the car."

As soon as Liam was gone, Seth sat down on the edge of the bed to catch his breath. What was he thinking? He should have opted for the 11th Street bridge. It would have been simpler. It probably wasn't too late. Movement in the closet startled him and he jumped. On the shelf above the hangers peered a gray furry head with distinctive black markings. Obviously, Mildred. Seth sat perfectly still

The Mistaken Haunting of Seth Harrison

looking at her. Mildred stood on the shelf staring back. Seth was starting to panic again when Mildred made a move. Perching on the edge of the shelf, she launched herself a solid five feet over and down onto the bed. Seth was impressed.

"Wow. That was pretty good, ya know, for a cat." Mildred turned her nose up as if in indignation. Seth leaned toward her. Mildred didn't move. He leaned further. Seth got close enough to reach out and offer his hand. Mildred stretched her neck out and allowed a modest scratch to the head.

"So much for warming up to me. Is this your room?"

Mildred let out a small *meeuuuw*.

"Sorry for kicking you out. Maybe I should just go." As if in reply, Mildred jumped down and began weaving her way through his legs, purring loudly.

"Um. Okay, maybe not." Just then, Liam came through the door with two boxes from the car.

Noticing the cat he said, "Okay. So much for playing hard to get, Millie." Then, he looked up at Seth. "It seems she likes you already."

"Yeah, I guess."

"Pizza's on its way. Let's go sit down and talk about some ground rules."

Seth braced himself. Here we go, he thought. The hidden agenda. "Sure. Now that I'm here, let the rules begin." Seth grabbed his bags and headed out to the living room.

"No. Wait. Not rules, really. Bad choice of words. Just talking about how we, together," Liam emphasized the statement with two hands pointing back and forth at Seth and himself, "are going to make it work. As you might have noticed, I'm a bit of a collector."

Marie LeClaire

Seth looked around. "So, that's what you're calling it?"

"I know it looks bad, but I'm going to work on cleaning things up. In the meantime, please don't move things around. There is a method here." Liam looked around at the clutter. "Or at least there used to be," he said weakly.

"Yeah. No worries." Seth picked up a short piece of rusty chain on a table near the couch. "What is all this stuff?"

"Let's just say I have an interest in orphaned kinds of things."

Seth glared at him.

"Oh! No! Another bad choice of words. No offense. Not you. Just random things that don't appear to go with anything else." Liam waved around his house nervously. "See?"

Seth, satisfied with the apology, lowered the chain back onto the table beside half of a broken ceramic bowl.

"What's the point?"

"I look for things that might have a certain value."

"Like antiques or something?"

"Something like that. On the weekends, when I can, I go to a few estate sales to see if I can find anything interesting."

"Wow. You must not have a lot of friends." Seth pushed aside an old crocheted blanket and plopped down in one of the upholstered chairs.

"*Meeeooorrooowworrrr.*"

"Oh, stop it, Millie. Seth will be staying with us for the time being. Let him be." Liam turned to Seth. "Millie has taken a liking to that particular afghan in just that spot."

The Mistaken Haunting of Seth Harrison

"Sorry, Millie." Seth made a move to get up.

"Don't be silly." Liam held up a hand. "Millie will deal with it, won't you?"

"*Mmrrww*," Millie said as she planted her rear end on the carpet and put her nose up in the air.

"We'll all have to make a few changes."

The doorbell rang announcing the arrival of pizza.

"*Mmmww*."

"Yes, Millie. Of course, there's peperoni."

Chapter 6

When Liam got home from classes at UMass, Seth was already there, sitting on the patio drinking a Dr. Pepper and staring out at the hedges that bordered the yard. It looked like he was talking to someone.

Liam slid the glass door open to the patio.

Seth jumped.

Liam didn't see anyone else around. "Sorry, buddy. I didn't mean to startle you." He leaned against the jam. "So, how was your first full day at The Lube?"

"Depressing."

"It'll get better."

"Maybe."

"At least things are going okay here, right? We probably should check in on that."

"Oh, God. That sounds like a hospital meeting," he moaned.

"Yeah. I suppose it did."

"Yeah."

"I just want to make sure things are okay, you know, your first full day at work and all."

"Yeah. Can we eat first?"

"Sure. I've got beef stew in the crock pot. No guarantees on how it's going to taste. I've never been much of a cook."

Liam headed into the house and around the corner out of sight in the kitchen. He was filling two bowls when he heard something on the patio. Listening closely, he could hear Seth mumbling under his breath. His first thought was *Oh, great. The kid really is crazy*. Then he stopped to listen as Seth spoke in a hushed voice.

"Shit. Really? I thought you were gone. Leave me alone."

Liam peered around the corner to see Seth, hands covering his eyes.

"Hey, Champ. What's up?" Liam stepped out of the sliding door onto the patio just in time to see two ghosts, a young man and a young woman in Victorian era garb scoot behind a neglected juniper hedge, leaving a vapor trail in the breeze. Liam looked back at Seth who didn't return his gaze.

"Ah, it's nothing," Seth glanced over to the edge of the yard.

The ghosts peeked over the hedge just enough to see the two humans. Liam and Seth watched. They appeared to be arguing with each other.

Seth slid his eyes sideways to see Liam looking over at the ghosts too.

"You can see them?" he asked cautiously.

Liam hesitated and decided on honesty.

"Yes."

"But how? Is it some kind of shared hallucination? I've heard about that."

"Not exactly." Liam was unsure where to go from here.

Seth paused, waiting for more. When nothing was forthcoming, he got a little irritated. "Then what *exactly* is it?"

The Mistaken Haunting of Seth Harrison

"It's complicated."

"It doesn't seem that complicated. You either see my hallucination or you don't."

"Yes, I see them and it's not exactly a hallucination."

"What do you mean it's not a hallucination. Of course it is." Seth's face reddened. "It's the same thing I've been seeing for years. It's what put me in the nut house in the first place."

"Yes, I understand that and I'm sorry that it had to go that way."

"Go what way? What are you talking about?" Seth's voice was getting louder. The young ghosts were peering intently now watching the conversation.

Liam spoke slowly, "I see them because they are really there."

"Now who's the crazy one. You should take a few of my pills."

"Seth, I know this sounds unbelievable but those two apparitions are real."

Seth looked at him suspiciously. "I'm starting to think that the cardboard box under the bridge is a better bet." He got up abruptly, knocking the chair backward, and headed inside to collect his things, keeping one eye on Liam who followed him into the house.

"Wait. Let me explain. Then, if you want to go, I won't stop you."

"You couldn't stop me if you wanted to."

"Okay, agreed. Just give me ten minutes."

"You got five."

Liam was feeling a little desperate. He wasn't expecting the ghosts to show up at his home, at least not so quickly. He wasn't prepared. He played it all wrong but he couldn't let Seth walk out the door. He had too much riding on this.

"Please, at least sit down." Liam gestured to the sofa. Seth looked out at the ghosts behind the shrub looking at him and moved away from the window.

Liam took a seat on the arm of the adjacent chair. This had to go well. He leaned on his knees, took a breath and began.

"I can see your hallucinations because they are not figments of a disturbed brain. They are ghosts, apparitions, spirits, whatever you like. You are not hallucinating. You are being haunted."

"You're out of your mind."

"Am I? How do you explain it?"

"Unremitting something..." Seth threw his hands up. "I don't know! I'm not a doctor."

"Seth, there are things in this world that are not easily explained by science. Ghosts are one of them. I've seen ghosts before, not these two, but others. I've seen other things too. Right now, it's important that you consider the possibility that you are being haunted."

"Okay, let's say I am, which I don't believe. Why are these two ghosts haunting me?"

"I don't know. Ghosts can't talk to humans."

"Seriously? What, they're not allowed?"

"No, not forbidden. They simply can't communicate that way."

"Terrific."

"I've known they have been haunting you for few months now."

"And how did you know that?" Seth felt his anger rising. Here it was, some really bizarre hidden agenda.

The Mistaken Haunting of Seth Harrison

"I have a certain sense of things. I see things other people don't. Not ghosts necessarily. Everyone can see them. It's just that ghosts are very sneaky and avoid being seen. I can sense other things."

"Like????"

"I see auras. I can tell if things have a certain energy to them that might indicate something supernatural." Liam paused to let the information sink in. "And I can sense people that have special abilities, skills that can be misunderstood as mentally unstable."

"What are you saying?"

"I'm saying that you are not crazy. You are one of those individuals that has the gift."

"A gift!? That's what you're calling it! Well, aren't I freakin' special?"

"I think you see doorways, portals, distortions in time and space." Liam was talking fast now. "They look like a shimmer or a play of light about seven feet across."

"Shut up! You're creeping me out." He got up from the chair and started pacing erratically.

"What I'm trying to say, Seth, is that you are not crazy. You are gifted. The medications haven't resolved any of these things, have they? That's because they are not caused by a mental illness. They cannot be chemically corrected."

"SHUT UP!" he shouted.

Liam remained silent.

"So, let me get this straight. You think I have a gift. You have known for months that I am not hallucinating and have said nothing? You let me go on thinking that I'm crazy and have let me take medication that I hate for no good reason? Is that about it?"

"I didn't have any alternative, Seth. The doctors wouldn't have believed me even if I had come forward."

"You could have come to me. You could have told me!"

"I was concerned I would make things worse."

"Worse than what? Growing up in a nut house thinking I'm a freak? Although now I'm just feeling like a different kind of freak. I don't even know if this *conversation* is real."

"Seth, you have a gift."

"Yay for me!" Seth had had enough. His brain was on fire and he needed time to think. He ran into his bedroom, grabbed his jacket and headed for the door.

"Wait! Where are you going?"

"I don't know. I need to think." The door slammed behind him.

Chapter 7

Seth had no idea where he was going. His brain was spinning out of control. He needed to get away from Liam, or more specifically what Liam had told him. He needed distance, and lots of it. He needed to know he was free to do whatever he wanted, come or go as he pleased.

The bus stop was just around the corner. According to the sign, the number thirteen bus ran this route until 12 am, four hours from now. That's when he'd have to decide if he was coming back or not. He was starting to worry that Liam would catch up with him when the Number Thirteen came around the corner. He hopped on, flashed his pass and took a seat behind the driver. His nerves settled down gradually as the distance increased from Liam. As he watched the streets go by, the names turned to numbers. He remembered what his friend had said about 11th Street and Jefferson. At the time, he considered it a joke, but now it seemed worth checking out. 20st St. 19th St. 18th St.

"Hey, does this bus go to 11th Street?" he called to the driver.

The driver looked into his mirror for the source of the question.

"Yeah. You want off there?"

"Yeah. How close is it to Jefferson?"

The driver looked at him suspiciously.

"Three blocks."

"Thanks. Let me off at 11th then, please."

Two minutes later, the driver pulled over and opened the door.

"Be careful, son. There's some strange people down there."

"Yeah. I know. I might be one of them," he said as he hopped down the stairs and headed in the direction indicated by the driver.

At first glance it looked like any other intersection, traffic lights, cars, noise. He wasn't sure where to go or what he was looking for. Then he saw them, makeshift tents in a little camp, shopping carts filled to overflowing with bags of unknown treasures. The stench didn't hit him until the wind shifted. Did people really live like this? The scene shocked him out of his own troubles for a moment as he realized that he was just a step away from life on the streets. He was trying to figure out his next move, when a voice surprised him from behind.

"New here, huh?"

Seth spun around to see a pretty girl about his age standing uncomfortably close to him. She was remarkably clean considering the surroundings.

"Yeah. I guess. You, ah, live here?" He took a step back.

"Not really. I just come here when I can't stand my foster family any more. I'll hang out here for a day or two then go back."

"Don't they worry?" Seth knew the answer but felt obligated to ask anyway.

"They don't care one way or another. They get paid whether I'm there or not."

Seth looked at his feet. "Yeah. I spent some time in foster care."

The Mistaken Haunting of Seth Harrison

"Really? How'd you escape?"

"I didn't exactly escape. I aged out, but not before I spent the last year at Bridgewater."

"The prison?" The girl's eyes got big and she took a few steps back.

"No! The Department of Youth Services sends the crazy kids there."

"Oh." She took a step back toward him. "Are you crazy?"

"Depends on who you ask."

"I'm asking you."

"I thought I was, but now I'm thinking that maybe I'm not, but if I'm not then there's some weird shit happening to me."

"I know the feeling," she said, rolling her eyes and nodding.

"My name's Seth."

"Nice to meet you, Seth. I'm Brit. Short for Britany."

Their eyes connected and lingered for a moment before they were interrupted by a yell from across the yard.

"Hey Brit. Who's that?" asked an angry middle-aged man with a scruffy beard. He was wearing too many clothes and pushing a shopping cart over the potholed dirt terrain.

"No one, Nick. Just a friend."

"You know it's by invitation only around here."

"No worries. He's not staying," she called back.

"Invitation only?" Seth looked at her in disbelief.

"Yeah. It's one of a few camps where people look after each other. They're very particular about who stays here."

"Seriously?" The surprise in his voice offended her.

"Yeah. Is that so hard to believe?"

"No. Not at all. Look, I don't even know what *I'm* doing here."

Brit smiled and waved at another resident while she talked. "Well, what *are* you doing here?"

"I guess you could say I'm running away from home."

Brit let out a laugh. It made Seth smile despite himself. She took him by the arm and started walking.

"Let's keep moving so the natives don't get any more restless."

"Sure."

She led him down an embankment and along a footpath beside the drainage ditch.

"So, how crazy are you?"

"Up until a few hours ago, I thought I was full-on crazy. Now, I don't know." Seth kicked an old can down the path.

"What changed?"

"Someone told me that the hallucinations I've been seeing are ghosts."

"Wow. So, you're either crazy or haunted?"

"Yeah. I guess."

"Bummer." Brit kicked the same can further along.

"Yeah."

They both started laughing. He fell into an easy rhythm with Brit.

"If your hallucinations are two vapey-looking people in old clothes, I vote for haunted." Brit was serious.

"What?!" Seth looked around quickly. "You see them?" For years he was the only one that could see them and now Brit was describing them perfectly. What was happening to his world?

The Mistaken Haunting of Seth Harrison

"Not at the moment but I saw them earlier when you first got here. They were kind of following you, in a weird floaty way."

"Oh my God, that's them." Seth ran his fingers through his hair. "What is going on? How can you see them?"

"I've seen ghosts before. No one believes me though. That's what happens when you're a kid."

"So, I've been medicated for years and stuck in a nut house for no good reason." Seth gave the can a solid kick.

"Well, I don't know about that, but I do know there are ghosts following you." She was smiling ever so slightly, then she broke into a grin and gave Seth a jab to the arm. "All I know is that I see them too, whatever they are."

"Sometimes I think they're talking to me but I can't hear them." He watched Brit for a reaction.

"Did you ever talk back?"

"No! I don't want anything to do with them! I just want them to go away!"

"If they haven't gone away in years, my guess is they won't. Unless you figure out why they're haunting you."

"They aren't haunting me! They are hallucinations!"

"Okay, we're back to where we started." Brit traced a circle in the air. "Are they ghosts or not?"

"Well, if you and Liam can see them, I guess they're not hallucinations."

"Who's Liam?" Brit moved the can a few more feet with her toe.

"This guy who took me in when I turned eighteen."

"You got kicked out of the nut house?" Brit sounded a little concerned.

"Yeah. How's that for a low?"

Marie LeClaire

"Where's your family?"

"Dead."

"Hm. Sorry."

"Don't be." Seth walked past the can, leaving it on the side of the path. "It was a long time ago."

"So, what's Liam got to do with it?"

"Liam told me he knew for months that I was seeing ghosts and that I have some kind of gift."

"And?"

"I got freaked out and took off."

"No other plan?"

"Nope. I ended up on a bus that got me here."

As they were talking, a couple of teenagers appeared across the drainage ditch carrying backpacks and acting suspicious. They looked around nervously, slung the packs off their shoulders and reached in. Pulling out two cans of spray paint, they squared off in front of the large concrete wall that supported the bridge. Seth and Brit watched without a word. Just when the artists were about to commence, two slow streams of vapor traveled up the ditch, collecting into large clouds next to the young artists. Figures appeared out of the mist, one male and one female, both appeared to be in their early twenties. They looked directly at Seth and Brit.

"Is that them?" Brit asked.

"Shit. Yeah, that's them."

"I wonder why they're following you around?"

"I don't care." Seth waved his arms at the ghosts shouting "Go away. Go away."

The ghosts, standing behind the painters, started to wave angrily back at him, pointing and shouting words that couldn't be heard.

"Say something," Brit whispered.

The Mistaken Haunting of Seth Harrison

"Why are you doing this to me?" he asked almost pitifully.

The female ghost poked the male and then pointed at the artists who were about to begin their masterpiece. The teens, intent in their work, hadn't noticed the misty vapor behind them. Seth and Brit watched as the ghosts closed in on one of the teens and began pushing his arm as the spray paint started to flow. The second teen started arguing with him while the first started to panic as he continued to write. He struggled to stop but couldn't. The ghosts were in full view now, holding firmly to his hand. They all watched as the ghosts spelled out their message on the ditch wall.

HE KILT US

Seth was staring in disbelief. The young teens, completely spooked, ran for their lives as soon as they were able. Brit inched away from Seth ever so slightly.

"Well, that explains a lot," she said.

"Brit, you can't be serious. You believe that?" He pointed at the wall where the two ghosts stood proudly and boldly in front of their work, arms crossed, chins high.

"Brit, they're ghosts. Look, they're probably from a hundred years ago. How could I have killed them? And if I did, don't you think I'd know who they are?"

"I don't know," she replied doubtfully. "Maybe you're a ghost too."

"Really? Come on! I'm no ghost." Seth slapped his chest repeatedly to indicate his earthly nature.

"Alright. Maybe not. And maybe you didn't do it." Brit eased up a little.

"I didn't. Trust me."

Meanwhile the ghosts were standing on the other side of the ditch pointing aggressively and nodding their heads.

49

Marie LeClaire

"Why do they think you did?"

"Believe me when I tell you I have no freaking idea."

Brit looked closer at the apparitions. "Are they covered with blood?"

Chapter 8

Liam was pacing back and forth in his living room smacking his forehead with his palm.

"Way to go, champ!" Smack. "You should have thought this through. You knew it was coming." Smack. Seth was going to be his bargaining chip with the Consortium, a way to get under their skin, make them talk. He needed to find him. Fast.

Mildred wandered back in through her cat door.

"Mrrrouwwww."

"He's gone."

"Mmmeeeooooowwww hhsssss."

Liam sent her a glare. "Yes, Millie, I know. You were right. Are you happy?"

"Mmrroew."

"I don't know where he went," he barked angrily. "If I did, I'd go get him."

Mildred jumped onto the arm of the sofa, her head turning side to side as she followed him.

"Mrrww. Mmreeeooowrr."

"Yes. He is unusual. It's like he has an extra aura. I'm not sure what it means yet but I've done some reading and the lore references the Openers as having a *second shadow*."

"Mmmrrreeeeoooww."

"Hard to say. No one alive has ever seen an Opener. The book also references someone with more power than just an Opener, called a Link Master." Liam walked over to the old oak hutch and unlocked the glass door. He pulled out a thin leather-bound book. "Where was I seeing that?" He flipped through the pages. "Here."

He followed the text with his finger. "There are stories of a royal line of Link Masters that trace their lineage back to the origin of the Links. Although there have been none specifically identified as such, some stories would indicate that they exist or existed at one time. Link Masters can not only open and close links but also create them."

"Mrrwwow"

"No, I won't say anything until I'm sure. Do you think I'm a fool? ...Don't answer that." Liam was pacing the dining room. "Do you think he knows more than he's letting on? He must know something. Surely his parents gave him some clue about what he is. Is he just playing with me? And he's wearing something around his neck. I haven't noticed it before. I don't think he wore it at the hospital."

"Meeoooowww."

"Yes. That's what I thought. But it's not just one of those trendy trinkets the kids are all buying. He keeps it hidden in his shirt."

When the phone rang, he spun around and ran to the living room, tripping over a cannon ball next to the couch.

"Ouch. Hello? Seth?"

"No. Who is Seth?" It was Marilisa Samstone. She was as close as you can get to the Consortium Council without actually talking to one of them.

"No matter at all, Marilisa. What a pleasure to hear from you." Liam smoothed over his shirt as if she could

The Mistaken Haunting of Seth Harrison

see him. "How can I help you?" He did his best to be cordial with the Councill. They had information about his father. He knew they did. His father had been on a Consortium *errand* when he disappeared.

Marilisa scoffed at the ingenuine greeting. "It's not much really but we need someone to take on a task and your name came up."

"I might be available. What do you need?" Mildred meowed from the couch, tipping her nose up and doing the best eye roll she could manage.

"Shush," Liam whispered.

"Are you talking to me?" It was almost an accusation from Marilisa.

"No. Of course not. Just talking to the cat. What is it that you called about?"

"Hm. We need a little research on a possible Link reported to be somewhere near Fall River, Massachusetts."

That got Liam's interest. "Yes. That's just down the street from me, relatively speaking. What do you have on it?"

"The counsel was reviewing one of the transcripts from the Lizzy Borden trial..."

Liam interrupted her. "Well, there's some light reading."

She ignored him. "Nevertheless, they noticed a reference to a relative who appeared to be in two places at the same time. It seems somewhat Link-like and certainly the circumstances might imply otherworldly influences. They'd like it checked out if you have the time."

"That's an interesting spin on the story and it could explain things."

Anyone who lived within a hundred-mile radius of Fall River knew the story well. Lizzy Borden was charged

Marie LeClaire

with murdering both her parents in their Fall River home in the late 1800's. The trial was a national sensation. She was acquitted of all charges but many people thought she was guilty. The story lives on today as a local legend, with many paranormal claims added over the years.

"Do you have time to follow up on it or not?"

"Yes, of course. Send me what you have and I'll run it down."

"Fine. Expect the email by morning."

"And my usual fees apply."

"Yes, of course, lest anyone think you act for the good of all. Let me know when you find something."

Liam had taken up his father's passion for the Links and other things unexplained. His research, however, and his allegiance, was well outside the Consortium oversight. It was a stale mate of sorts. They shared limited information with him and he shared limited information with them, unless they were paying for it. Unbeknownst to the Consortium, he had similar arrangements with the King's Legion. He had barely hung up the phone when Mildred let out a howl.

"Yes. She's not my biggest fan, is she? Still, this could be an important find. I want Seth on board for this one. Let's see what he can do. Where is he!"

Marilisa hung up the phone at Consortium headquarters, a modest office suite on the grounds of University of Michigan in Ann Arbor.

The Grand Chairman, Fay Wolfenstien, looked up briefly from the manuscript she was studying. "Thank you

The Mistaken Haunting of Seth Harrison

for taking care of that, Marilisa. Was Liam able to help out?"

"He's always able, even eager to be helpful. He makes me a little uncomfortable that way."

"He didn't press for any further information?"

"No."

"Liam has never given us any reason to mistrust him."

"I know. Just a feeling, is all."

"Well, I hope he can find something in Fall River." Fay made a note in the margin of the transcript. "Here. See that Liam gets this by morning."

"Yes, of course. Will you be heading out there yourself?"

"No. I have to get some lecture notes together so I can follow up on an old legend out of Tombstone, Arizona." In addition to running the US branch of the secret Consortium, Fay Wolfenstein was a U.S. History professor. Her position included guest appearances at universities and museums around the country. It allowed her to travel easily, asking questions of locals without raising suspicion.

"Tombstone? Does it have to do with the famous shootout?"

"Indirectly."

Marilisa hated being kept out of the loop. After all, she was more than just a secretary. She was the Executive Secretary to the Grand Chairwoman of The Linkage Consortium Council. If she was going to do her job properly, she needed to know things. Fay was always tight with information, so Marilisa pushed the issue.

"There's been a lot more investigating lately. Is there a problem in the Linkage?" "

Marie LeClaire

Over the last three hundred years the Consortium had been creating and maintaining a data base that includes, among other things, the location and status of Links, access points to a mysterious network of dimensional portals unseen by most humans, with Liam being one of the exceptions to the rule.

"One more Link was lost to the King's Legion last month. I don't like it."

The King's Legion had been gaining control of the open links by placing an unholy beast at the portal. No one alive could open or close a Link, thanks to the Legion's murdering spree, so they maintained control over them by stationing these creatures on one side.

"Secured by a Guardian?" Marilisa asked.

"Yes, I'm afraid so. Poor soul." Fay shook her head.

"Yes, indeed. Do you know who it was?" Marilisa asked. She made the Catholic sign of the cross. The zombie-like monsters, created through the ritualistic killing of a human, held blind allegiance to the Callers of the King's Legion, and anyone who held a Caller Coin.

"No. It might not be a new one, it could have been moved from another location."

"I hope that's true."

"Yes. I'm anxious to see what Liam finds in Fall River."

Chapter 9

Brit and Seth were staring, transfixed by the activity on the other side of the ditch.

"What's happening now?" Brit grabbed Seth's arm.

"How do I know?" Seth replied without turning away his gaze. As they watched, the female ghost seemed to faint, or fall, or melt really, into a vapor puddle. As she was going down, the male ghost swooped in, literally, and scooped her up.

"Is she okay?" Brit asked with concern.

"I don't know. I've seen that happen before. Then they just vape away."

Sure enough, as Seth was talking, both ghosts turned into vines of vapor and whisked away on a nonexistent breeze.

"See. There they go."

"Will they come back?"

"Sooner or later. But usually not for a few days."

"Where do they go?"

"Again, how do I know! Until a couple of hours ago, I thought they were just hallucinations, remember!"

"You don't have to get snippy." Brit flashed him a pouty face.

"Sorry. I'm a little freaked out by the whole thing."

"What are you going to do?"

"I don't know. Should I go back to Liam's? It's starting to appear that he's right." Seth was feeling a little embarrassed by his initial reaction.

"Maybe he is, but I have a lot of questions about that. Like how long has he been seeing ghosts and what's in it for him?"

"Wow, trust issues?"

"Don't you?"

"I guess. I'm trying not to think about it. It's not like I have anywhere else to go at this moment."

"You can stay here."

"Under the bridge?"

"That's my plan. If I go home now, I'll just get the shit beat out of me. If I wait till tomorrow, maybe not."

"That's harsh." Seth winced.

"Welcome to my world."

"Why don't you come back to Liam's with me?"

"Sure. Like he's going to say 'Oh great! A teenage runaway! Come on in! Let's have a party!"

"If he does have some kind of secret plan, then he wants me back. So, he'll have to take the package, at least for tonight."

Brit hesitated.

"Come on. It can't be worse. And if we don't get going, the buses are going to stop running." The sun had set hours ago and night shadows were being cast by streetlights.

"Sure. Why not."

Liam jumped up from the living room chair when he heard the door open.

Seth poked his face around the edge of the door.

The Mistaken Haunting of Seth Harrison

"Hey, Liam." He waited to enter, feeling like he needed to be asked in.

"Hey Seth, come in, come in." Liam waved him in.

Seth came just inside the room then stepped sideways to reveal Brit standing behind him and waited for Liam's response.

"Got a new friend, I see." Liam's voice did not hide his irritation.

"In a way, yeah. She saw them too." Seth thumb-pointed to Brit.

Liam took a moment to understand this development. "By 'them' you mean...."

"The ghosts." It was Brit who answered.

"I see. Well, this is interesting." Liam was quickly assessing whether this was a boon or a problem. Whatever happened, he didn't want to spook Seth again.

"She needs a place to stay tonight."

Liam looked back and forth at them. "Oh, NO! She cannot stay with you. If this is some kind of adolescent booty call, it is not happening."

Brit and Seth looked at each other with shock. It hadn't occurred to them what this might look like. They both turned bright red with embarrassment and started talking over each other.

"No. No. Not like that." Seth explained.

"Oh, definitely NO! What kind of girl do you think I am?"

Realizing that he was about to blow it again, Liam held up his hands. "Okay, wait. Sorry. It's just that...well... Look, let's start again?"

Brit and Seth let out an awkward chuckle.

"Yeah, I think we better." Seth nodded and paused, collecting his thoughts. "When I took off earlier, sorry

Marie LeClaire

about that, I ended up un... well, wandering around and I met Brit. Brit this is Liam. Liam - Brit.

"Hi." Brit waved a hand from the doorway.

Liam nodded her way.

"So, while I was talking to Brit, the hallucin...I mean the ghosts showed up and Brit could see them plain as day."

Liam turned his gaze directly at Brit. "Really? And you didn't run screaming in the other direction?"

"I've seen ghosts before," Brit explained.

"I see." This was getting more interesting to Liam by the minute.

"Anyway, we had a talk about it and she made me think more about what you said."

"You realized that I may be right." Liam tried not to sneer as he said it but he wanted to get the upper hand here.

"Maybe that." Seth wasn't ready to admit total defeat. "So, anyway, Brit needs a place to stay tonight. Can she sleep in my room and I'll take the couch?"

"I don't know yet. But certainly come in." Liam waved them into the living room. "I'll warm up pizza, unless you've already eaten."

"No. We're starving." Seth looked to Brit for confirmation. She nodded.

As Liam headed to the kitchen, Brit looked around at the oddities that passed for décor.

"This is all a little gothic, don't you think?"

"Yeah, and there's more stuff you can't see. Liam's a *historical researcher*. He's got a thing for old useless stuff." He picked up a rusty fireplace shovel. "Kinda weird."

The Mistaken Haunting of Seth Harrison

Brit wandered over to the dining room table and reached for the book Liam had taken off the shelf earlier. Mildred came out of nowhere, jumping onto the center of the book and letting out a wail.

"Whoa!" Brit jumped back. "Who are you?"

"That's Millie," Seth explained. "She's a bit of a character."

"Yes, she is." Liam said as he headed over to the book. Mildred stepped aside as he picked it up. "It's a rare edition and really shouldn't be handled," he explained as he replaced it in the cabinet and locked the glass door. Then turning to Brit, "So, Brit, what's the reason you have nowhere else to be?"

"I have a foster family that doesn't really care if I come or go so, sometimes I go."

"I see. So, is someone looking for you? Has anyone called the police?" He knew it sounded creepy as soon as he said it, as if he was trying to determine if she'd be missed if some misfortune was to befall her. Brit looked at him strangely.

"I'm just wondering how much trouble I'll be in by harboring a runaway for the night." he explained quickly.

"They're not looking for me. They know I'll be home soon enough."

"And my door has a lock on it," Seth offered. Both Liam and Brit looked at him. "I'm just saying. I found a key on the windowsill in there and it fits the door. I didn't mean anything by it."

After an awkward silence, a ding was heard from the kitchen. Relieved for the interruption, Liam got up. "Ah, that would be the pizza," he said as he headed back to the kitchen.

Seth walked over to Brit and spoke quietly. "Really, he's okay, just a little weird sometimes."

"Yeah, a little." They both giggled.

Chapter 10

They were seated around the table, finishing off the pizza when Seth brought the conversation back around to recent events.

"Liam? What's happening to me?"

Liam looked at Brit and then back at Seth. "Are you sure you want to get into this tonight? It can wait till tomorrow." He didn't need another teenager complicating things.

Seth caught the unspoken question. "It's okay. I don't care if Brit knows."

Liam looked at her and hesitated. She did appear to be an OP, a Sensitive maybe. She had a faint glow. Maybe it was her age. He'd never meet a young OP until Seth.

Seth insisted, "As of now, she knows as much as I do."

Liam relented. "It's a little complicated," he began, "I'll tell you what I do know." Liam paused for effect and to collect his thoughts. He blew this once already and he didn't want a replay of that. Mildred was sitting close by on her blanket, now resting atop the ottoman, to make sure of it.

"I am what's called a Sensitive. That means that I can see things and sense energy that the average person can't."

"Like ghosts?" Seth asked.

Marie LeClaire

"No. Everyone can see ghosts. We just don't look for them or we excuse them away as plays of light or low blood sugar or whatever. And ghosts are very elusive unless they want to be seen. I've spotted your ghosts before at the hospital but when they saw me seeing them, they disappeared quickly."

"How did you know they were *my* ghosts?"

"I didn't, at first. Then I started noticing them more often and paying attention to who was around. More than once, I saw you staring straight at them, so I knew you saw them too."

"Who are they?" It was Brit's turn to get a question in. "And why do they think Seth killed them?"

"What?" Liam stopped short. He looked back and forth at them, waiting for an answer. Brit turned to Seth, hoping she hadn't said anything wrong.

"Well, we were down at 11th and Jefferson." Seth recounted the story of meeting Brit and walking under the bridge. "They used a kid and a can of spray paint to write a message on the wall by the overpass. It said HE KILT US. They kept pointing at me, really angry like."

"Then what happened."

"The two teenagers ran like crazy, just about wetting their pants." Brit started to giggle.

Seth smiled along with her. "Yeah. That was pretty funny." They both spiraled into a giggle fit. Even Liam gave up a grin before moving on.

"Alright. Alright." Liam waved his hands to calm them down. "Then what happened."

Seth continued, "Then the woman kind of fell and the man scooped her up and then they vaped away."

"Yes, as I suspected. When a ghost moves something in our world, it takes great energy. It must have taken both of them to write the message."

"Yeah, now that you say that, they were both moving the spray can along," Seth nodded.

"Yeah," Brit confirmed.

"Ghosts get their energy from some *thing* or some *place* in this world that was important to them in their lifetime. It's called a touchstone. They would have gone back to it to rest and recharge."

"Do you know where they went?" Seth was getting drawn in despite his initial resistance. The fact that Brit seemed to believe it easily might have been a factor.

"I have no idea. It's impossible to tell. They can travel around pretty easily up to a certain distance unless they're using Links." Liam intentionally let the statement sit. He wanted to see Seth's reaction. Seeing no indication that he knew anything, Liam waited for Seth to ask for more information when he was ready.

Seth took the bait. "What's a Link?"

"Links are portals that take a person or a ghost to another place directly, without having to travel the distance. Magical doors in a way. They look like a gray fog and they shimmer. Only Link Openers and Sensitives can see them as far as anyone knows, and ghosts of course. Openers can lock or unlock them." Again, Liam mentally cautioned himself to take it slow.

"Those gray shimmery things you mentioned?" Seth asked.

"Yes?"

"I can see them," Seth admitted.

"Yes. I thought you might," Liam nodded.

Seth paused. "Does that make me a Sensitive?"

Marie LeClaire

"Sensitives see auras, energy fields around people and things. Like halos. Do you see those?"

"No."

Liam took a long breath to slow himself down. If Seth wasn't a Sensitive, what was he?

"Then you are an anomaly. Someone who can see Links but not a Sensitive."

"Then I'm an Opener," Seth concluded.

Liam was very cautious. "You might be. I'm not quite sure at this point." If this kid was an Opener, that changed the whole game in both the Consortium and the Legion.

Seth shook his head slowly, trying to take it all in.

"I must be a Sensitive like you," Brit blurted out.

"What?" Seth turned to her.

Liam studied her, trying to decide if she was telling the truth. Mildred chimed in with a long MMEEOOOOW, and walked straight over to Brit. She rubbed her head against Brit's arm resting on the table.

"Yes, Millie. I know you know." It was Brit who spoke, reaching out to give Mildred a scratch.

"And a cat Sensitive too?" Liam asked surprised. "Any other animals?"

"Strangely, squirrels, but they don't usually have a whole lot to say. And they talk really fast about nothing." She crinkled her nose as she spoke.

Seth shook his head back and forth before he spoke. "Wait. Are you saying that you both talk to animals?"

Brit offered an explanation. "Not talk exactly. More like understand."

Seth leaned over, putting his head in his hands. "This has to be some giant hallucination."

"I know this is a lot to take in," Liam didn't want a repeat of earlier today. "Maybe this is enough for one

The Mistaken Haunting of Seth Harrison

night. It's almost midnight anyway. Why don't we all get some sleep and talk more in the morning."

"That sounds great," Seth agreed quickly.

"Okay. Brit sleeps in your room, you on the couch...and I mean it." Liam looked at them both.

"I don't need to knock Seth out of his bed," Brit protested. "I can sleep on the couch."

"No way." Liam and Seth responded in unison. Liam wanted to give the girl her privacy. Seth replied out of gallantry, puffing his chest out a little. There was no way he was going to take the bed while a damsel in distress slept on the couch.

"Okay then. Bed it is." Brit got up and turned towards the door indicated by Liam.

Seth jumped up. "Wait!" He almost fell over himself getting to the bedroom door. "Ahhh, let me go clean it up a bit."

Forcing themselves through the Link, James and Sarah, collapsed on the floor of the collections room at the Salem Heritage Museum. They weren't quite back to home base yet but already they were feeling more energy. They slipped under the door and slowly floated out, low to the floor, up the stairs and through the halls. They headed straight to their touchstones. The permanent display, titled Leisure Time in Victorian America, included a fiddle and a washboard among other musical instruments of the day. Their vapor began to reform as they leaned up against the wall just below the tableau.

"That was far too long away this time, James," Sarah sighed as a wispy strand of her vapor drifted through the

Marie LeClaire

glass doors protecting the exhibit, and encircled the washboard.

"Indeed. We should not do that again," James agreed as he attached himself to the fiddle.

"Let's not." They both lay, phasing in and out of a vaporous state, recharging now that they were home. These instruments had been theirs in life, more than a hundred years ago. The fiddle was polished up nicely but the strings were just for show, too loose to be playable. The washtub was there, minus the tin thimbles Sarah had used to play it. What did it really matter, anyway? They couldn't actually touch them.

"It appears we finally got through to that good-for-nothing Seth that we know what his kin did to us," James huffed out.

"Indeed, we did. He didn't react as I thought he might, though." Sarah fanned her face with her hand.

"Yes, what do you suppose that was about?" James closed his eyes and tilted his head back.

"Probably didn't want to upset that young girl that was showing him unseemly attention."

"She hardly was, Sarah."

"Nonetheless, she looked a bit loose to me, if you know what I mean." Sarah looked down her nose.

"I say it takes one to know one."

Sarah swung an open hand in the direction of James' head which turned to vapor just before impact.

"Ouch, woman. What'd you do that for?"

"Well," Sarah hesitated, "for being right I suppose."

They both started laughing. They had regained a more defined, if still translucent, appearance. Now able to get up and float around with ease, they took advantage of the empty museum to stretch their misty legs, walk/floating

The Mistaken Haunting of Seth Harrison

down the halls and through the exhibits, into the research section where old books and periodicals were stacked.

"Too bad we can't read, Sarah. There might be something in here worth knowing."

"Yes, James, you've said as much before."

"Well, after a hundred years there's not much new conversation to have now, is there?"

"No, James." Sarah made no effort to hide her lack of interest.

He tried a different tact. "What do you suppose is up with young Seth? He acted like he didn't know what we were talking about."

"I can't say. Except that maybe it wasn't Simeon after all. I just can't imagine he could do it."

"Sarah, are we going to have this conversation again? I know it was him who killed us. It had to be. There wasn't anyone else around. Remember when Sour Puss helped us read about it? The newspapers all said it was him."

"Now that we're getting closer to the revenge we need to move on," Sarah waived a hand through a row of books, "I'm having second thoughts. He really is a nice boy. And what if we're wrong? There never was any direct proof."

"Oh, no. You're not going all soft on me now. First, it was that we can't kill him because he was just a young one. So, we hang around for six years and now we can't kill him because you don't think his kin really killed us. Sarah, we've been planning this for a hundred years!"

"I know, but now that he's grown, it seems more real. We *have* been following him around for a long time and, I guess, maybe I have gotten a little fond of him."

"All I know is once he's dead, we're dead, finally."

"How are we going to do that exactly, seeing as we can't lift anything?"

Marie LeClaire

"You know how. That old ghost from the cemetery said we can just grab his no-good stone-cold heart and hang on till it stops beating."

"And when do you plan to do this?"

"Me? Why does it have to be me? You can do it just as easy, you know."

"Me? I'm a girl. I don't do such things. That's your job."

"Mine? Oh, I get it. You're sweet on him, that's why. Just like you were sweet on Simeon when we were alive."

"I was not."

"You sure were. You thought I didn't notice it, but I did. Can't say I blame you. He was a righteous soul, except for the thievin' murderin' part."

"I was not. Even if I was, what did it get me? Just as dead as you. So, if killing Seth sets the record straight, then that's what we need to do."

"*We*? You already said you weren't going to be the one, so what you mean is *me*. I don't think you want me to do it at all. You're sweet on him just like you were sweet on Simeon!"

"I am not."

"You're-sweet-on-him. You're-sweet-on-him." James bated her with a sing-songy voice.

Sarah wound up and took another swing at his head. James vaporized and her hand passed through the smoke.

"Ouch. Hee hee. It was worth it." James continued to snicker as he floated down the hallway, humming his tune.

Chapter 11

Seth woke to the sound of Liam in the kitchen making coffee. The L-shaped floor plan put the kitchen just out of sight.

"Doc, you gotta make so much noise?" Seth called from the couch. He smashed the pillow over his head and moaned.

"It's impossible to silently make breakfast." Liam was not apologetic. "It's time to get up anyway. It's 8:30."

"Are you kidding?! I'm a teenager!" Seth yelled from under the pillow.

"That won't help you here," Liam called back. "Rise and shine."

Seth let out one more moan before surfacing. "Is Brit up?"

"I heard some rumblings from the bedroom so, I'll say yes."

Just then the bedroom door opened and out came Brit, cleaned up and dressed, long yellow hair twisted into a knot and held in place with a pencil. "Good morning," she said cheerily.

"Oh, brother," Seth rolled his eyes.

"Good morning, Brit. Coffee?" Liam offered.

"I'd love some, thank you."

Liam poured her a mug and placed it on the counter between the kitchen and dining area. "Cream and sugar are on the table."

Brit headed over to fix her coffee as Seth dragged himself into the kitchen. "I'd love some coffee. Thanks for asking."

"How did you sleep, champ?" Liam poured another mug and handed it to Seth. "It was a crazy day for you yesterday."

"Don't remind me. I was kinda hoping that it was all a bad dream." Seth rubbed his eyes, "except for you." He smiled in Brit's direction. "I just can't believe that all these years I haven't really been crazy at all."

"Weren't there times when you knew or at least thought that maybe something else was going on?" Liam prompted.

"Sure, but I was always reassured by grown-ups that I was, in fact, crazy, no matter how real things seemed. One time I thought that the ghosts knocked something over in my room. They didn't believe me and I was in trouble twice, once for knocking it over and once for blaming it on the ghosts." Seth paused in thought. "Can ghosts do that?"

"Yes, much like they did with the spray can yesterday. They can move things in our world but with great effort. Technically, they can talk to us too. But, again, it's with great effort and it still might be too mumbled to understand anyway, so they usually don't even try."

Brit slurped on her coffee. "How did you learn so much about … all this?"

"I've picked up on things over the years."

Brit suspected there was more to it than that, but Seth interrupted before she could call him on it.

The Mistaken Haunting of Seth Harrison

"When did you know you were...you know...different?" Seth asked.

"I started noticing things when I was a teenager. That's when most of us start to have different experiences. It appears to be part of the hormone package of adolescence."

"How come no one thought you were crazy."

"My parents were already involved in a way. My father was a Sensitive, too. He became obsessed with the Links. My mother did her best to understand him."

"Is it hereditary?" Seth was firing off questions now.

"No. I don't know how it works exactly. I don't know if anyone does. What are your parents like, Brit?"

"Hard to know. My mom's a drug addict, running around in Hartford last I knew. My dad, well...Let's just say, hard to know." Brit got quiet.

Liam took the focus off Brit. "Seth, what about yours?"

"I don't know much more than Brit, really. They raised me till I was ten but I don't remember much. They were killed by intruders."

"Right. I remember reading that..." Liam stopped himself before he made reference to the hospital file. "You don't know anything about their attackers? Like who they were or what they wanted?" Liam was fishing. He'd read that Seth's parents were tortured and wanted to know more. Clerics from the King's Legion created Guardians by brutally murdering people. If Seth's parents were somehow involved with Links and other magic, maybe Seth knows something he doesn't know he knows.

Seth got up with his dirty dishes and headed to the kitchen area. "No! I said I don't remember, alright?"

"Sure, Seth. No problem."

Marie LeClaire

There was an awkward silence. Brit changed the subject. "So, what's up for today?"

Seth was glad for the subject change. "I have to work at 11. Liam, do you think you can drive me in? I don't really feel like taking the bus today."

"Of course. I can drop Brit off somewhere at the same time." He turned to Brit for confirmation.

"You can drop me off around the corner from my foster house. If you drop me out front it will require way too much explanation." Brit rolled her eyes.

"Got it. No problem. Let me know when you're ready."

James and Sarah were charged up and ready to hit the road again. They were down in the basement of the museum, in the collections area, headed for the Link. Their eventual destination was the cemetery in Fall River. Sarah dragged her hand over some of the more beautiful items like jewelry and fancy clothes. She loved floating through them. She would step right into the manikin and pretend she was wearing whatever delicious dress was hanging there.

"Come along, Sarah. We haven't got all day."

"I know, James. But must you always rush me?"

"Must you always dawdle?"

The Link was at the far back wall of the collection space. The closer she got to the Link, the worse she felt. After passing all the beautiful things, the items turned dark. Here were the things that people generally didn't want to see or touch. A noose, allegedly from the last hangings of the Salem witches dating back to 1692. Beside it was a pair of nylon stockings allegedly used by the

Boston Strangler to kill his last victim in 1964. *Who keeps these things,* Sarah wondered for the millionth time.

"This part is so disturbing to me, James. I wish we didn't have to go past these things every time we wanted to travel." It was a familiar complaint. When you've been tied to someone for a hundred years, there's not a lot new to say. Still, James comforted her.

"I know. Just float by really fast and look the other way. Think about butterflies or something happy."

"Yes. Thanks for reminding me. That helps."

They made it to the back wall where they hovered for a moment waiting for the Link to come clearly into view. Slowly a shimmering gray orb appeared against the wall and then a window opened in the center revealing a view of Bridgewater State Hospital.

Chapter 12

James pointed to it. "There it is. You go first."

"Why do I always go first?"

"You don't always go first."

"Do so."

"Do not."

"Do so." Sarah stood with her arms crossed over her chest, nose in the air. She wasn't going to let him off the hook.

"Maybe you do. Look, these things give me the heebie jeebies. And I hate that feeling of being pinched by some giant fingers. So maybe I put it off as long as possible."

"There now. That wasn't so hard, was it?"

"Now will you just go."

She didn't complain as much as James, but squeezing through these Links was no picnic and cost a little extra energy.

Sarah took a deep breath, which means nothing for a ghost, and stepped through the Link. Instantly she was in the back of the hospital property near what used to be the farm.

She looked around quickly to see if anyone was watching. And not just for humans. Even though you could see through the Link window, you could never be completely sure what you were getting on the other side. Occasionally, there were Guardians. Sent by the King's

Marie LeClaire

Legion to guard the Link. Guardians killed first, asked questions later. If she saw one, she would pop back through quickly to the other side. She was sure this was the real reason James never went first. With a quick look she determined that it was all clear and waved James through, which he did, wafting in just a few steps to her right. From there they were on their own to get to Fall River. There was another Link that would take them there, but it had been locked for decades.

"Tell me again why we're doing this." Sarah didn't disguise her irritation as they floated out to the main road. They usually tried to hop a car, vaporing into the trunk to hitch a ride. It was a little tricky though. You could never be sure where they were going and if you weren't paying attention, you'd end up bailing out on the highway which was very risky business. Technically, you couldn't kill a ghost but if you blasted their vapor into a million pieces, it was a long and painful process to reassemble. Getting hit by a car would do the trick. Buses offered a more predictable ride but less convenient, stopping in a dozen places between here and there.

"We need to talk to old Sour Puss," James explained, "about the day we died. You got me thinking, about Seth acting like he didn't know what we were talking about."

"Finally, you listen to me."

James mocked her with a puckered-up face and wagged his head side to side.

"Better late than never," Sarah rolled her eyes. "Let's get this over with." It took a few car hops but eventually they made it the twenty-five miles to the cemetery. It was an old place, established in 1885, and was most famous for the graves of Andrew and Abby Borden, victims of the

The Mistaken Haunting of Seth Harrison

most notorious murders in Massachusetts history, and their daughter, Lizzie, the main suspect in their deaths.

They looked around for Sour Puss. He didn't exactly guard the place, but he kept a close eye on what happened on the grounds and always greeted travelers promptly. Nothing happened at the cemetery without him knowing about it.

Sour Puss was the eldest elder among the cemetery ghosts and held an unofficial leadership role. His given name was long forgotten even by him, or so he says, and his current moniker referred to his disagreeable disposition. He kept things calm when the dearly departed, that's what ghosts call themselves, got out of hand, which was more often than you would think. The last ghostly dustup was two days ago when a discussion of the Links got heated. The Legion's control of them, using Guardians to restrict passage, was always a topic. The dearly departed relied on the Links to move about easily. Some thought they were seeing more and more of this control and felt that an alliance with the Legion would ensure their continued access for traveling and visiting ghost family. The alternative was to side with the Consortium in the hopes of some earthly protection. The Legion were well-known to be heartless and brutal. Their opponents referred to them as the evil that came before evil. The Consortium, on the other hand, were considered to be too passive and secretive and thus unpredictable.

"There he is." Sarah spotted him first. Initially just a vapor tentacle rising from behind a gravestone, the mist quickly formed itself into a large round man with a hole in his chest. His puffy sleeves and bloomer style knickers indicated an era long ago in Europe. Puss didn't remember when he was born or died. He'd been following his

Marie LeClaire

touchstone, a broach of the family crest, around for hundreds of years. He and the broach arrived in the New World in 1635 with one of his descendants who was promptly killed in a tavern brawl. The broach was sold a few times and eventually buried with its last owner, attaching him forever to Oak Grove Memorial Park Cemetery.

"Well, we haven't seen you around these parts for a while now. Still out looking for your killer's kin?"

"Not anymore. We found him a few years ago with a group of kids touring the museum in Salem." James stood up a little taller as he bragged.

"Maybe." Sarah interrupted.

"For sure," insisted James.

"I'm just saying, things don't all align." Sarah interrupted.

Sour Puss rolled his ghostly eyes. "Did you come here because you wanted an audience for your argument?"

"No, no. Sorry Puss. A hundred plus years with the same woman can wear any man down to squabbling."

Sarah swung at him, leaving a momentary hole in his arm.

James winced.

"So, is this visit business or pleasure?"

"A little of both," Sarah continued, while James reconstructed his arm. "It's always good to see you and to keep up on current events. We try to keep informed but there just aren't that many departed in our neighborhood and they don't like to travel much. What's the latest news?"

"It seems to be the general opinion that travel through the Links is becoming more limited by Guardians. The assumption is that the Legion is responsible but there is no direct evidence to that."

The Mistaken Haunting of Seth Harrison

"Of course it's the Legion. Who else could it be?" James was adamant.

"That's the question, isn't it? Who else?" Puss stroked his beard, leaving a short vapor trail that quickly reverted back to its original appearance.

Sarah was keeping a cooler head. "Do you think there are more powers at play than the Legion and the Consortium?"

"Anything is possible," Puss replied. "After all, look at us, standing here dead, having a conversation about unexplainable things."

"True," James said calming down slightly. "I keep forgetting that."

"In any case, how can I help you two move on?" It was a common greeting among departed. If a ghost could either make amends or avenge their past, they could leave the ghostly world for the next place, wherever that was. Or they could choose to stick around but without the burning desire to take action against those who wronged them in life.

"We want to know more about Simeon Harrison."

"Ain't that the kid that killed you?"

"Yes," Sarah agreed, "and maybe."

James shot her a look.

"I don't know what you think I can tell you. What do you want to know?"

"Like how do we know if he's really the one that killed us?"

"I can't answer that! How would I know? I was in the Links when you died." The phrase meant a vaper was traveling. "You're not sure it's him?"

James hesitated so Sarah jumped in. "No, we're not. We have found his descendant, Seth Harrison, but he doesn't seem to know anything about us."

"Well," Puss barked, "it has been a hundred years. Maybe your story wasn't one of those that got passed down at the holiday dinner table!"

"Maybe, Puss," James admitted. "But I have to tell you that when I look at the young man, I don't have that burning desire to kill him. I have the burn, just not to kill *him*. We've been putting it off until the boy turned legal age, not that it matters to killing, but neither Sarah nor I could bring ourselves to kill a boy."

"Exactly how long have you been following this lad around?"

"Six years."

"Great Cesar's ghost! What are you waiting for?"

"Puss! He was just a boy!" Sarah argued.

"So, you've been telling yourself that it'll be better to kill him when he's a man? Is that it?"

"Well, yeah," James agreed. "I guess it doesn't make much sense when you say it like that." He paused to think. "But like I said, I just don't feel the burn to kill him. What do you make of that?"

"I don't pretend to know everything, James. Certainly not what you need to do to move on."

"Figuring it out is making my head hurt." James put both his hands on the sides of his head and squeezed it into an elongated shape.

Puss' voice softened. "I'm sure I don't know about who you should be killing or not. What I *can* say is that you probably should be sure about it, otherwise it might work against you."

The Mistaken Haunting of Seth Harrison

"To that end," James held up a ghostly finger, "we came to find out what you remember from that newspaper article you read for us a while back, about our murder."

"Bless me, James. That was a hundred years ago." Puss scratched his head.

"I know, but you have a good brain. You can remember."

"I remember that people thought it was Simeon but no one actually saw him do it. The departed that were here sensed trouble and stayed out of sight. Why are you asking?"

"We told Seth that we knew Simeon killed us and he pretended like he didn't know what we were talking about."

"What do you mean *you told him*?" Puss raised one eyebrow and leaned in. "You talked to him?"

"Not exactly. We made this kid paint it on a big wall." James said.

"Impressive."

"Thank you," Sarah added so as not be overlooked for accolades. "It took both of us and we were wiped out afterwards."

"And creative too." Puss added with a nod to Sarah who beamed a translucent blush.

"So, we're starting to wonder if we've been wrong all these years. Truth is we were sleeping when we were killed. We just assumed it was Simeon that double-crossed us for the money."

"I'm afraid I don't know any more than you do, well, about this at least," Puss chuckled.

Offended, James pushed his shoulders back. "What's that supposed to mean?"

Marie LeClaire

"Let me know how it goes," Puss called as he vaped back the way he had come.

Chapter 13

"Where did you learn how to make pancakes, Seth?" Liam called from the kitchen.

"YouTube."

"Nicely done," he replied.

Brit mumbled as she stuffed the last bite into her mouth. "Yeah. They were great."

Seth shrugged it off. "You guys are easy to please."

"It's true that I don't have the most discerning palate," Liam agreed.

Seth looked at Brit and rolled his eyes, eliciting a giggle.

Liam looked up, wondering what the joke was. "Seth, what do you say you come along with me on some research today?"

"Can Brit come?"

"I don't know. Brit, can you come?" Brit had made a habit of staying over at Liam's on the weekends. The men relented to her insistence that she sle3p on the couch and the house had quickly become her home away from foster home.

"Sure. No one's gonna miss me. Where are we going?"

"We're going in search of a Link."

Brit and Seth looked at each other. Seth asked "What do you mean by searching for a Link?"

Marie LeClaire

"I received a call last week from someone close to the Consortium Counsel. One of the members has been looking over some old manuscripts and found a record that looked odd about a person being in two places at once. They know I'm sensitive to the Links so they asked me to offer some assistance. It would be nice to have you along. I'm guessing you can spot a Link a mile away." Did Seth know the extent of his gift?

"I don't know about that. I just know about the two at the hospital." Seth admitted.

Liam dropped a pan in the sink. "What do you mean two?" It never occurred to him that there would be a second Link so close to each other, so he never looked.

Seth jumped at the loud bang and looked at Liam. "I think I saw what you're describing on the grounds at Bridgewater. I didn't pay much attention. Hallucinations, remember?" Seth half smiled.

"Yes, of course." Liam was trying to remain calm. "Do you remember where you think you saw them?"

"I don't know. Not really. There's one out near the old garden. That's where I used to see the ghosts a lot. I think the other one was on the other side of the grounds somewhere. I saw it when I was looking for an escape plan. I can't believe I'm talking about this like it's all real."

"I assure you, it's all quite real."

"Does this mean I don't have to take that damn medication anymore?" Seth perked up at the realization.

Liam had forgotten all about the antipsychotics prescribed to Seth at discharge. "I can't tell you what to do about that, but it appears to be unnecessary to me." Liam was cautious here. "Do you know if there's any withdrawal to worry about?"

The Mistaken Haunting of Seth Harrison

"We can look it up online," Brit chimed in. "I look up my meds all the time."

Seth's coffee mug stopped half way to his mouth. "You're on meds?"

"For ADD. I don't think I have it. I think I'm just distracted by the stuff I see that others don't."

"Like talking squirrels?" Seth let out a teasing smile.

"Yeah, like that." She feigned irritation. "And I think I've seen that thing near the old garden."

Liam and Seth both turned to her.

"I might have spent a few weeks there one time, in between foster homes."

"Anything else unusual out there that either one of you would like to share?"

"Not me." Brit looked over at Seth.

"I think I remember one Link was less shimmery, harder to see."

"Yes. That one was probably locked. Openers can lock and unlock Links," Liam explained.

"How do they do it?"

"I don't know. I've never seen anyone open one before. There hasn't been a known Opener around for a long time but according to my research, it's different for each person and has to do with waving your hands around."

"Where do you get all this *research?*" Brit asked.

"Oh, I pick up things here and there. As you can see, I have a lot of unusual material. My father left me quite a lot as well." He made reference to the many closets and book shelves lining the walls.

"What do you mean *left you*?" Seth asked.

Liam stumbled a bit. "My father was devoted to the Consortium. He traveled all over the world hunting down

Marie LeClaire

information for them. When I was sixteen, he left in search of a Link in Nova Scotia and never returned."

"Oh no," Brit held her hand over her heart. "What happened?"

"No one knows. Or at least no one is saying."

"You think someone knows?" Seth asked.

"I've always thought the Consortium knows more than they're saying. When he didn't come back, the Consortium turned their backs on us." His voice was bitter. "They left my mother in financial and legal ruin." A blank stare come over his face.

Brit turned the conversation back to the present. "Let's look at what he left you. Can any of that stuff help us find the link today?"

"I'm sure I can't put my hands on it easily." The opening of Links was information he had come across doing research in the Legion archives. When he had gotten stonewalled by the Consortium on circumstances of his father's disappearance, he had contacted the Legion for information. The more he interacted with the organization, the less he liked them, and the further entrenched he got. When he started to limit his time with them, veiled threats were made.

"And we have three pairs of eyes," Liam indicated the group with a sweep of his hand, "to take with us. I'm sure that will be more than sufficient."

Mildred, who had been listening intently to the conversation from the living room, made her presence known, jumping up on the counter with a *Mmmrrrrroooooooowwww*. Liam reached for a plate and poured her a saucer of milk.

Seth shook his head. "I feel like a freak. I don't like being…whatever it is that I am. I just want to be normal."

The Mistaken Haunting of Seth Harrison

Brit had a different take. "I've known I was different for years. I've been too afraid to say anything until now. I don't feel like a freak. I feel like I found my tribe. I'm finally normal, or as close as it gets anyway."

"I'm sorry, Brit. I didn't mean it like that. You've known who you are all along. I'm just trying to figure it out. Overnight I went from being crazy to being weird. It's like I have to get to know myself all over again."

"Sure. I get it," she said, not at all offended.

"Look," Liam said. "We're all in uncharted water here. I don't know about how a lot of this works either," which was true. Despite his association with both the Consortium and the Legion, information had been doled out sparingly. He'd rather align with the Consortium, but they weren't taking him seriously, keeping him at arm's length by withholding access to any of their files.

The Legion had offered to take him into the fold if he brought them something useful. Their black-marketing network through the Links was extremely profitable. But the risk of dying was considerable.

"So why don't we take it one step at a time," Liam continued. "Who's up for a road trip?"

"Shotgun!" Brit shot her hand high in the air.

They headed out to the car with Liam in the lead. Brit leaned into Seth. "What's with the coat?"

"He thinks it's cool."

"Hm," she nodded slowly. "I see why he lives alone."

They caught up to Liam at the car. "So where are we going exactly?" Brit was buckling herself into the passenger seat of the Mercedes. Seth was slouching in the back, hoping to catch up on some sleep, as they pulled out of the driveway.

Marie LeClaire

"Fall River. A little town on the Rhode Island border best known for its textile mills and shoe factories at the turn of the last century. Now, it's known for its most infamous citizen, Lizzie Borden."

"Oh my God! You're kidding! Really? We're going THERE?" Brit could not contain her excitement.

Surprised by her reaction, Liam inquired "Yes. Are you familiar with the story then?"

"Who isn't?"

"That would be me," Seth waved a hand in the air with little interest.

Brit immediately launched into the old rhyme.

"Lizzie Borden took an axe
Gave her mother forty whacks
When she saw what she had done,
She gave her father forty-one."

Brit turned to Liam. "*That* Lizzie Borden?"

"Yes, that would be the one."

"Really? That story's true?" Seth piped up.

"Yes, it is. And we're starting our research at the house where it happened." Liam was happy to see their interest.

"Wasn't that a really long time ago?" asked Brit.

"It was. 1892. A hundred and twenty-five years ago, give or take."

Seth and Brit looked at Liam, surprised that this knowledge seemed to roll off his tongue.

"I've been reading transcripts from the investigation and trial all week. Sadly, I know everything there is to know about it, which just attests to my complete lack of a social life."

The Mistaken Haunting of Seth Harrison

"I didn't want to say it," Brit said.

"It's true though," Seth agreed.

Brit asked, "What exactly are we looking for?"

"Hold up a minute." Seth raised his hand in the air. "I'm not as well informed as you both seem to be, so could someone back up and fill me in on the basics?" Seth was almost pouting.

"Well," Brit started rattling off the story at squirrel speed. "Lizzie had this really mean father and stepmother who were probably abusing her and her sister. So, one day, Lizzie had had enough and went out to the kitchen and got the small kitchen axe they had for chopping the heads off chickens. She went upstairs, whacked her stepmother like a hundred times, then went downstairs and did the same to her father."

"Really?" Seth looked to Liam for confirmation.

"Basically, yes. She was tried and found not guilty of the crimes but most of the town believed she did it."

"But we don't?" Seth asked.

"Well, there were a lot of unanswered questions at the time. There still are. In particular, there is a report that a man named Morse – Lizzie's uncle from her biological mother who died when she was just two – was in town that day. There is also a report that he was at the home of a friend in Salem which would have been half a day's ride on horseback. The only way he could have been in both places at nearly the same time is if there were a Link nearby. It's not uncommon for Links to be associated with unexplained phenomenon or gruesome violence. They can have a strange effect on humans."

Seth put his head back on the headrest and closed his eyes. "This is starting to sound like a wild goose chase.

Marie LeClaire

How much of any of this stuff is still around? That was all a hundred years ago?"

"Oh, the house is not only around, it's open to the public as a bed and breakfast."

"What's that?" It was Brit's question.

"A hotel of sorts. You can stay the night in one of the rooms if you want, for a fee of course, and have breakfast in the dining room. *Bed* and *breakfast*."

"Okay, that's creepy." Seth looked disgusted while Brit was excited.

"Wow! Cool! Can we sleep there?"

"Not at $300 a night." Liam was clear on that. "But we can take the tour of the crime scene, every hour on the hour, for a mere $18 each."

"Yippeee. Link hunting is going to be fun." Brit was doing a little dance in the front seat.

Seth was in the back, shaking his head.

Chapter 14

An hour later they pulled up in front of Lizzie Borden Bed and Breakfast Museum in Fall River.

"Wow." Brit couldn't stop staring. It was prettier than she'd expected considering two vicious murders had taken place here. As they were parking in the driveway, a group of tourists came out of the back door, led by a docent in period costume.

"Hey, that's just like what my ghosts wear," Seth noticed.

"*My* ghosts?" Brit pointed out.

"Well, they kinda are, I guess."

"Interesting that you noticed that, Seth. It helps us date whatever happened to them. When we're done here, we can try a little research into other notable events around that time. Who knows? We might find something."

"Yeah, that'd be great...I think."

"First, let's catch the next tour."

Thirty minutes later, the tour guide was leading their group around to the parking lot in front of the barn.

"This is where Lizzie, according to one version of her statement, was when the murders took place. Sitting right up there," the guide made a gracious gesture up to the eaves of the barn, "eating pears that were picked from trees on the property. Other statements put her in various parts of the house, which is one of the reasons that she

Marie LeClaire

came under such scrutiny by the police. Her uncle claims to have seen her from that window." A grand wave of the other arm indicated the top floor of the main house. The guide now looked like a giant Y.

Seth and Brit looked at each other and rolled their eyes as they exaggerated the guides gesture, then started giggling.

Oblivious to the ridicule, the guide continued. "Another story says that her uncle was not in town at all. Family in Salem testified to him being home with them on that day."

She turned and led the group into the barn. "The Bordens were a very affluent family and as such would have had several horses and carriages that would have been stored here. After the murders, the property was abandoned and fell into disrepair. The barn was just recently restored and these are some of the items they found during the renovation." Another arm wave drew attention to a display on the rear wall consisting of general farm tools of the day. The gesture elicited more giggles from Seth and Brit. They glanced over at the wall and were about to head out of the barn when something caught Seth's eye. A few weeks ago, he would have called it a hallucination, but now he lived in a different world, a world where strange things happened. He nudged Brit and pointed to a small metal object hanging on the wall behind the tour guide. She saw exactly what he was looking at, an eight-sided coin about the size of a half dollar. It was covered in crud and tarnish but beneath the mess, it looked like it had something in the center. More noticeably, it gave off a slight shimmer around it like a halo. If not for the darkened barn, they might not have noticed it at all.

The Mistaken Haunting of Seth Harrison

Liam saw it too and, by the look on his face, it was something important.

"Now, if you could all follow me back to the house, we'll enter the kitchen and see where Lizzie supposedly burned a dress two days after the murders. And we'll see an axe that the authorities believe is similar to the murder weapon. Of course, the actual murder weapon was never found."

Liam reached out to Seth and Brit, taking them firmly by the arm, encouraging them to stay back. As everyone else left the barn, they stepped into the shadows so as not to be seen staying behind.

As the barn door closed, the light got even lower. Liam tugged them to the back of the barn to the display wall. He was tense with excitement, looking over his shoulder and scanning the upper levels for surveillance cameras.

"Liam, what is it?" Seth asked in a hushed tone.

"I think," Liam looked around nervously, "it's a Caller Coin."

"What's a Caller Coin?" Brit whispered back.

"I'll explain later. Right now, I need you to hop the railing and pull it off the wall." He was looking at Seth.

"What? You want me to steal it!?"

"Yes, now! Hurry, before we're missed."

"Why don't *you* steal it?" Seth argued.

"Just go get it!" Liam's voice had a cool angry edge to it. "I'll watch out for the guide," and he headed towards the front of the barn.

Seth looked at Brit who shrugged her shoulders. Seth slid over the railing and reached out for the medallion. It glowed slightly brighter when his hand got close to it. Seth turned to Brit who noticed it too. He turned back to the

Marie LeClaire

small piece of metal. It was nailed securely to the wall. He looked around for something to pry it off with.

"Hurry up!" Liam commanded harshly.

"I'm trying. Brit, look for something."

Brit scanned the artifacts and spotted a hammer further down that was suspended between two nails. "Right there," she pointed.

Two large strides took Seth to the hanging tool. It clanked against a nearby garden spade as he lifted it off.

"Be quiet, for God's sake!" Liam growled at them.

Quickly, Seth pulled one of the two nails out and the medallion tumbled into his hand. The other nail took a little longer to work out.

"Now!" Liam growled again from the door.

He stashed everything into his coat pocket. With two more strides, he replaced the hammer. He was just swinging back over the railing when the guide opened the barn door.

"You can't be in here. You have to stay with the group," she admonished them.

"So sorry. My niece loves horses and she just wanted to take an extra minute to look around." Liam had turned on the charming smile of an indulgent uncle.

The guide turned toward Brit. "I'm sorry, honey but you can't hang around here without a guide."

"Oh, that's okay. I understand," Brit played along. "Sorry about that."

"No problem. Just come along now to the kitchen."

As the guide escorted them to the house, Seth thought he felt a strange pulse coming from the coin. He wasn't sure if he could believe it or not. His heart was racing and he was sure his face was red. He looked around guiltily as they entered the kitchen.

Liam saw Seth's distress and moved toward him, putting a hand on his shoulders to steady him.

"Good job," he whispered. "Hang in there. We'll be out of here in a few minutes."

Chapter 15

"Okay, Liam. Can you please tell me what I just stole?" They had barely pulled away from the curb. Seth's heart was still racing, his anxiety skyrocketing. "I've never stolen anything in my life."

"Really?" Brit asked in disbelief.

"Well, not that I can think of right now at least," he snapped.

"Wow."

Seth was approaching panic. "We just stole an artifact from a museum dedicated to two grisly murders and that's what surprises you?"

"Well, yeah, kinda."

"Stop it, both of you." Liam's stern voice halted their banter.

"Liam, what's going on?" Seth insisted.

"If that's what I think it is, we have just rescued a very powerful piece of magic from a third-rate museum owned by idiots."

"What are you talking about?"

"The item in your pocket is called a Caller Coin."

Seth slowly pulled the trinket from his pocket, opening his palm to reveal the coin and two nails. It glistened softly leaving a tingling sensation on his palm.

Brit was leaning over from the front seat gazing at it. "Why did you take the nails?"

Marie LeClaire

"I figured it would be harder to notice it was missing if the nails were gone, too."

"Good thinking for a first-time thief," Brit said, impressed.

Seth didn't know if he should be flattered or offended. "Yeah. Thanks."

"So, Liam, what does it do?" Brit asked.

"It doesn't *do* anything. It gives the person in possession of it control over Guardians."

"What is a Guardian and why do we care?" Seth turned the coin over in his hands.

"Guardians are monsters that the King's Legion uses to do their dirty work. They've been using them to guard the links, restricting passage. The creatures are simpleminded but strong and agile. They blindly follow the commands of anyone in possession of a Coin."

"They sound dangerous."

"Only as dangerous as their owners."

"I didn't know people could own the Links," Brit said.

"They can't. I was referring to the Guardians. People own Guardians."

"What? Like slaves?" Brit turned back to the front to look directly at Liam.

"Well, I'm not sure that's the analogy. More like you would own an animal, a very dangerous animal," Liam continued. "The only way Guardians come into existence is by very powerful magic wielded by a Legion cleric. There are only a few known to exist with such abilities. It is considered a dying art."

"How do they create them?" Brit kept at him with questions.

"By ritually torturing someone to death."

The Mistaken Haunting of Seth Harrison

"WHAT?" Seth was sitting bolt upright.

"In the death ritual, a Guardian is bound to the person conducting the rite."

There was silence in the car for a long moment. Brit and Seth looked at each other then back down at the medallion.

"So, did this belong to the Bordens?" Seth was putting the pieces together.

"I presume it did. Which explains at least a few things. Owners of Caller Coins have generally aligned with the King's Legion, most are full Legion members. In most cases, they are using the Links to traffic illicit contraband of some sort. Among other things, Guardians are used to block Links from being used, except by those cleared by their owner or on Legion business."

"And what are the other things?" Seth asked as he turned the coin over. He wasn't sure he wanted to know.

"Personal protection for their owners, taking care of interlopers or innocent people that stumble on the Link…"

"You mean killing them?" Brit asked.

Liam hesitated again. He didn't want to scare them off, but they needed to know what could happen. "In some cases, yes."

Seth shook his head. "Can we talk about something else for a while."

"Yes, please," added Brit.

1892

Chapter 16

"Now then, let us have our story straight one more time."

"Damn, Simeon, how many times shall we go over it. You think we're dull?" James was already irritated. Sleeping on the ground for a week had made him long for the Boston lockup.

"Did you consider that I was going over it for me, not for you?"

"Oh. No." James thought about that for a minute. "Are you dull?"

"Dull for getting mixed up with you two."

"What? I shall not be lumped in together with either of you." Sarah feigned offense. "For the record, here is our story. I became with child and my ma threw me out. My aunt in Virginia said she would take me in. You two are cousins that agreed to escort me there safely."

"Perfect, Sarah," Simeon winked at her. "You have that belly secured in place?"

"I do." Sarah tapped some stuffing she had wrapped around her middle.

"We shall go, then." Simeon led the way back onto the main road. The day was hot and the road was dusty, so they would certainly look like weary travelers by the time

Marie LeClaire

they got into town. Their scams had worked beautifully in Boston, but people there were becoming wary of street cons and the local cops knew them by name. They decided to work some of the outlying towns till things cooled off in Boston. The plan was to beg a place to stay for the night, maybe a barn or something, belonging to a wealthy family. They would sneak into the house, steal what they could, and get out of town. Tonight's stopover was Fall River. They should be there within the hour.

"So, Sim," James asked as they walked. "Tell us again how you came to be traveling on your own?" James had heard the story a few times now but something about it didn't sound right to him.

"Well, it's not that complicated." Simeon had whittled some of the details out of his story, staying as close to the truth as he could. "My folks had some property north of the city for years, farming corn mostly. Fire wiped out the crop going on five years ago, leaving us poorer than dirt. They told me to go into Boston to find work. I was just sixteen then. So, I did as I was told, staying in the city for a few months before heading back to the farm. When I got back, there had been another fire, this time in the house, and my ma and pa were dead. My two baby sisters were sent off to relatives in New Hampshire. And now, here I am, running scams with two of Boston's finest."

"Two fires in the same year. What are the odds of that?" James asked, a little tongue-in-cheek.

"Yes. Imagine the mess. But we all have our own stories, have we not, James?" Simeon was desperate to change the subject.

"Yes, we do." There was a long silence. James didn't share his story much. Like many poor families, the older children were kicked out early, making way for the

The Mistaken Haunting of Seth Harrison

younger ones. James was the oldest of twelve and on his own by age fifteen, hustling the streets for spare change. It was a rough life till he met Sarah.

Sarah spoke up. "May I suggest that we stay focused on the current situation and reminisce later." She didn't want the conversation to get back to her. She hated talking about the past. Her mother died in childbirth when Sarah was ten. When her father remarried two years later, the new mother made her life miserable until Sarah finally ran away at age fourteen.

After competing for change on the same street corner in Boston, Sarah and James realized they could do better as a team than either one could do on their own. That was four years ago. They met Simeon three years later sharing accommodations at the South Boston jail.

"Yes, our current situation," Simeon agreed. "We make a good team, the three of us, regardless of how we got here."

They crossed into the outskirts of town feeling confident in their plan. Little did they know the hand that fate would deal them this day.

It was another thirty minutes before they made their way to the main commercial district where small shops provided all of the modern conveniences. Farmers were setting up their goods in an open-air produce market, backing horse-drawn carts up to their stands to unload produce for the day's shoppers.

There was a commotion as the group entered the square. A farmer was fussing with a disagreeable horse who bucked at the backward push.

"Git on back there!" the farmer yelled as he shoved on the bridle.

Marie LeClaire

"Hey, there old boy," James jumped in to help. He stroked the horse along the snout, calming him down quickly. "Now, nice and easy," James talked to the animal as he walked him back into the farmer's stall.

"That, sir, is quite a gift you have," said the old farmer.

"Yes," Sarah jumped in. "He has quite a way with all kinds of animals, but in particular, horses."

"I can see that. You from around here?" The farmer looked the group over.

"No, sir." James stroked the horse once more before stepping away. "We are passing by on our way to Virginia."

"Good Lord, that will take the rest of the year!"

"We have been blessed with the graciousness of others, praise the lord," James went into his *I'm a humble Christian* act, "and have been offered rides and day labor to ease the journey. We are hoping for a bit of work here in Fall River. Is there any direction you might offer us?"

The farmer looked them over again. "Andrew Borden is known for taking advantage of those down on their luck. He could probably find something for you – but he won't pay you much."

"Whatever he might offer, we will appreciate," James assured him. "Where can we find him?"

"That be his house over there." The farmer scowled and pointed to a large house at the end of the street. "He and his family own half the town, including the factories."

"You mean these?" Simeon tried to hide his excitement as he indicated two three-story brick buildings belching out brown smoke and rumbling from the noise of machinery.

The Mistaken Haunting of Seth Harrison

"Yes, indeed. He owns them both. This one producing cloth," the farmer raised a hand indicating the one closest to the square, "and that one," another wave of his hand behind him, "is metalwork. They're already set for day labor though. You will have more luck at the house. His wife is usually home. Go by the kitchen door and check with the maid, Maggie."

"Thank you, kind sir." Sarah flashed him a smile.

The farmer's face didn't flicker from his scowl. "I suggest you don't stay long," he mumbled as he turned to unload his wagon.

Sarah, James, and Simeon split up and continued to pick their way through the market, each stopping periodically to ask questions about the Bordens. The Borden family, they were told, had made their fortune providing uniforms and equipment for the union army, and some suspected to the South as well. Now they were taking advantage of the Reconstruction by supplying fabric and machine parts to the south.

"I did not find a single person that fancied neither Mr. Borden nor his wife," Sarah reported when the rejoined at the edge of the market.

"Nor I," Simeon seconded. "Although some were more charitable than others."

"All the more satisfying it will be, then, to swindle them," James added as they walked toward to Borden house.

They were met at the kitchen door by Abby Borden. It didn't take them long to get an offer of a night's stay in the Borden's barn for a day's work. "And, mind you," Mrs. Borden had admonished, "you're getting a late start, so you best work harder faster to make it up."

"Yes, ma'am," they assured her.

Marie LeClaire

"And stay out of the house."

"Yes, ma'am," they said in unison.

"And don't bother Maggie. She'll be washing windows all day."

While the young people were knocking on the kitchen door, Andrew Borden was finishing his breakfast with a cup of tea in the sitting room, and talking to his former brother-in-law, John Morse.

"You cannot cut me off, Andrew. It will ruin me. You know that."

"All I know is that your line of the business is no longer profitable."

John was pacing back and forth as Andrew sat calmly in his wing-backed chair. "It's no fault of mine that the damn Indians have all the guns they need. You flooded the market at the war's end."

"That is not my concern."

"Please, Andrew, let me find another market. I understand there is conflict brewing at the southern border."

"I am already following that situation with another supplier. And since you will no longer be using the Links, I must insist that you return the Caller Coin I gave you."

"Andrew, you cannot do this. I beg you. What will I do for my livelihood?"

"I am sure that is not my concern. Be grateful for the work I have given you for these twenty years, considering that any obligation ended with the death of your sister."

John's sister had been Andrew's first wife. She died in childbirth with her second daughter, Emma. The reference enraged John.

The Mistaken Haunting of Seth Harrison

"Fine then!" John fingered the Coin in his pocket. "Your precious Coin is upstairs in my bag. You shall find it in your desk drawer when you return from your rounds. But mark my words, Andrew. This is not over."

Andrew calmly placed his teacup in the saucer on the table beside his chair and got up for his midmorning rounds at the factories. "Good day, Mr. Morse," he said as he gathered his coat and hat and headed out the front door.

John Morse pulled the Coin out of his pocket. He turned it over, grasping it tightly in his fist. He was fuming mad. "Who does he think he is?" He mumbled. "If it weren't for me, the Legion would have taken his Coins years ago." He had smuggled weapons to the South for Andrew for years. It was his idea to move the business out west. The way he figured it, he was directly responsible for a fair amount of the Borden's wealth. Now this! To be shoved aside. He wasn't going to have it. He stared down at the Coin. Could he do it? Would he do it? He held it in a closed fist in front of his chest, and commanded, "Come." Instantly a tall solemn figure appeared in a black hooded robe.

"Guardian. Is Andrew in possession of his Coin?" He suspected he was not. Andrew had bragged that he had dressed it up with a few stones and given it to his wife as a gift. She had no idea what it was. Andrew had joked that she wore it out in plain sight on special occasions. Otherwise, she kept it in her jewelry box with other valuables.

The dark figure shook its head.

"Then do you answer to me?"

A nod.

Marie LeClaire

"And if I commanded you to kill Andrew, would you be compelled to follow orders?"

Another nod.

Abby Borden's shrill voice carried into the sitting room from the kitchen, startling John.

"Be gone," he commanded quickly, and the figure disappeared.

Abby came into the sitting room expecting to find Andrew still at home.

"Where is my husband?"

"Left on his rounds already, as I will be doing shortly. Are my nieces about?"

"I'm sure I don't care enough to keep track of them. I have some vagrants cleaning out the barn. Don't bother them for anything you might need. Get it yourself."

"Of course, Abby. Will you be staying home this morning?" It occurred to him to kill Abby as well. He would not feel any more badly to take Abby down along with Andrew. His nieces, Emma and Lizzie, had suffered at her hand over the years and their deaths would leave the bulk of the family wealth to them.

"I'll be visiting a sick friend, not that it's your business," Abby replied curtly, then leveled a glare directly into his eyes. "When will you be leaving?"

"Likely later in the day. Not to worry. I will not be overstaying my welcome."

"What welcome?" Abby sneered as she headed upstairs.

John waited for Abby to be out of earshot. Holding the Coin in front of his chest he whispered, "Come."

The Guardian appeared.

The Mistaken Haunting of Seth Harrison

"Kill Abby Borden. Quietly. I am sure there is something in the kitchen that is up to the task. Then return."

The Guardian nodded and disappeared.

A scuffle could be heard upstairs. Then the Guardian reappeared holding a bloody kitchen ax.

"Good. And barely a sound. She must not have seen it coming."

The creature shook his head.

"Return to the barn and when Andrew returns home, kill him."

***

The young people were directed toward the barn with a list of chores. The boys took up forking hay and shoveling horse manure while Sarah collected eggs from the chicken coop. It wouldn't have been much of a hardship if Simeon and James didn't have a strong aversion to physical labor. They spent a good part of the morning complaining to each other and dreaming about making it big.

"Robbing a train, Sim. That should be our next caper."

"Yes, if you want to die by hanging."

"We'll not get caught."

"You are not of your right mind, James. Keep shoveling."

"It is serious hot in here."

"And smells bad as well."

Even though the banter that went back and forth was lighthearted, Simeon was uneasy about this job. Something wasn't right. The barn seemed odd somehow. He stopped to look around.

"Are you noticing anything strange?" Simeon finally asked.

Marie LeClaire

"Yes, now that you mention it. I'm working harder than you. Oh, no, wait. That isn't strange. That is normal." James stopped to wipe sweat away.

"I am serious, James. I have a feeling that we are not alone."

"Now you are the one out of your mind. No one is in here but us."

"Still..." Simeon looked around again. Hay bales and horse stalls. Nothing more.

"The sooner we finish, the sooner we can get out of here, so if you please," James tapped Simeon's shovel with his own. "Get that thing moving."

Simeon got to work but he couldn't shake the feeling of gloom. He was having one of his worry moments, times when his belly tightened up and his heart raced. His body seemed to be buzzing from the inside. The crystal around his neck irritated him, which was usually a bad omen.

The crystal pendant was one of Simeon's few possessions, and he guarded it with his life. His grandfather had given it to him when he was eleven with specific instructions: to never take it off and never tell anyone where he got it. Grampa said he would teach him how to use it when he got older but then the bad things started happening. Then the day he came home and found his parents brutally murdered in their house and his two sisters hiding in the barn with Grampa. Barely alive from a heart attack, Grampa told him to run! Run like the wind! And so, he did.

"I will be glad to be out of here." Simeon looked around again.

"You know we are sleeping here, eh?" James pointed out.

"Maybe not. We'll see what Sarah finds in the house. In the meantime, I have collected a few things that we can take with us when we go."

"And where will we sleep if not here?" James didn't really care either way but he wanted a plan.

"There was a grave yard on the way into town,"

Before Simeon could finish, James was chiming in. "Oh, no. We are not sleeping in a grave yard!"

"Stop complaining. That is the one place we will not be bothered and I saw woods on the back side that will make for good cover.

"Damn, Sim. Why do you have to complicate things?"

"I am telling you, James, something is not right here."

"In any case, we have to wait for Sarah."

Chapter 17

Sarah made her way back to the kitchen door with an apron full of fresh eggs.

"Hello?" she called quietly. No response. Where was the maid? She crept around the corner of the house in search of her. She spied her, high up on a ladder, bucket and rag in hand, mumbling under her breath. Sarah ducked back around the corner before she could be noticed.

She snuck into the kitchen. Once inside, she looked around quickly for contraband. Spotting a loaf of bread that could be easily hidden under her dress, she stashed it behind the egg basket near the door, to grab later on her way out.

She listened intently for sounds of someone in the house. All seemed quiet. She grabbed a broom and started sweeping the floors as a guise should anyone surprise her. Moving quickly and quietly, she made her way up the back stairs and into the first bedroom. Jackpot. It appeared to be the master's room. Sure enough, there was a tin of cash under the mattress. Why did everyone hide it there? Next, she spotted some jewelry on the dresser. She envied rich women for all the pretty things they had. She stopped to admire the pieces laid out on a dainty dresser cloth. It wasn't practical to steal jewelry. It was too hard to unload. She indulged herself a moment to admire it. Lifting the lid on the fancy jewelry box revealed a stunning broach. It sparkled up at her as if it was charged by the sun itself.

Marie LeClaire

She knew it was trouble. Its absence would be discovered long before the cash, which was normally only accessed in times of need. Still, it was so beautiful. It took her only a moment to rationalize that its location in the bottom of the closed box might buy her a day or two before it was missed. Impulsively, she grabbed it along with three jeweled hair pins. Why not? They'd be gone by morning anyway. Stuffing the jewelry down her bodice, she tiptoed to the bedroom door hoping to search the other two rooms. Just before she crossed the threshold, she heard a noise. It was a muffled whack repeated several times. She froze and waited. The sound stopped. Terrified she would be caught, she peeked out of the bedroom. Seeing no one, she ran back down the stairs that led to the kitchen. She stuffed the loaf of bread under her dress on her way out and headed to the barn.

She found James and Simeon outside getting some fresh air. "We must go now! Quickly," was all she had the breath to say.

Simeon and James jumped to it without question.

"We have things in the barn." They headed back inside where they had created a small pile by the door next to their carpet bags. Once again, Simeon felt the worry come upon him. Was that a shadow he saw in the far back of the barn? Maybe. He didn't stick around to see more. Grabbing the sack of booty and their bags, they cleared out, closing the door behind them.

James led them behind the barn where they stopped for a strategy meeting. "What are you doing, Sarah? I was looking forward to a hay bed tonight." James balked.

"We must get out of here, now."

The Mistaken Haunting of Seth Harrison

"Follow me." Simeon headed down the alleyway. "I have been planning a quick escape all morning. I had a feeling..."

Simeon led them along the edge of the property, then into the next yard, then turned right between the houses. The tall shadows of the buildings helped conceal their movements.

"You go that way, Sarah. James, that way. We will meet two blocks over and one block down. That will get us out of downtown at least."

They did as they were told, meeting back up a few minutes later.

"You are not still going with the cemetery plan, are you?" James was leery.

"What????" Sarah looked stricken.

"We can hold up in the woods in the back. No one will be looking for us there."

"Certainly, they will not! Because it is a CEMETERY!" Sarah was incredulous.

"Really? Come on. What are you? Afraid of ghosts?"

"Yes!" James admitted. Sarah nodded adamantly.

"Look, we will be in the woods in the back, not near the graves. It will be the safest place for now. We can stay the night and leave in the early morning, heading along the river to avoid most of the town."

Neither Sarah nor James could come up with a logical argument against the plan.

"Right, then. We should just do it." James resigned himself, "since Sarah bailed out of the barn plan."

"Don't blame me! I was upstairs to check out the bedrooms when I heard someone in the next room. I got all goose pimples. Who or whatever it was was disturbing. What can I say? Something was not right."

Marie LeClaire

"It is of no matter now," Simeon commented. "We should find a spot out of sight until tomorrow in case people start looking for us."

It was early afternoon when they set up camp in a clearing in the woods. James took a few extra minutes to create a nice bed of pine needles and leaves. Not as nice as hay, but not as bad as bare ground either, or worse, granite, which cropped out everywhere. Once they were all settled, they took stock of their situation.

"Alright. What's for dinner?" Simeon asked.

"I grabbed these just before Sarah showed up." James produced six eggs from the chicken coop.

"I've been carrying this around for two days. Can we please eat it?" Simeon proffered a large jar of tomatoes from a previous caper.

Sarah reached under her dress for a loaf of bread and a roll of bills.

"You are amazing, Sarah," Simeon said. "Cash, and bread too."

Sarah smiled wide at Simeon's praise. "You boys would die without me."

"We did okay in the barn," James said defensively. "Sim ended up with some silver spurs that we can sell in the next town. And I liberated this prize. Ta Da!" James pulled out a small jug of hard cider.

"We certainly do make a good team. I managed to pick up a few trinkets from m' Lady's dressing room." Sarah pulled out the broach and three jeweled hair pins. She turned the broach over in her hands. "Isn't it beautiful? I have never seen anything like it." It was a large brass coin, about the size of a half dollar with eight sides. Two thin lines were etched around the edge and a

The Mistaken Haunting of Seth Harrison

red stone was secured in the center surrounded by decorative scrollwork.

"Sarah! What are you picking that stuff up for? You know it is no good to us. It will be miles before we can sell it." James shook his head.

"Maybe it is not for selling," Sarah said defensively. "A girl likes to have pretty things you know! Besides, Sim has his own bauble. Why should I not have something nice." She was referring to the crystal that hung around his neck. She noticed he never took it off.

Simeon fingered it through his shirt self-consciously. He didn't like being pulled into an argument with James and Sarah and he especially didn't like any reference to the crystal.

"Mine is a family thing," he explained not for the first time. Sarah's reference to the pendant reminded Simeon that it had been irritating him all day. He didn't understand how it worked exactly, but when it was acting up it usually meant something bad was about to happen.

Hoping to move on from this subject, Simeon started digging through their bag of possessions. "Who cooks tonight?" he asked as he pulled out their one pan.

Sarah stepped up immediately. "If you want it edible, that would be me."

"You never give me any credit for doing some of the fixin'," James complained.

"You are correct, James. I never do," she agreed.

Sitting around the fire after dinner, James broke open the cider and poured them all a drink. He and Sarah tipped theirs down quickly and James poured them another. Simeon didn't take to the stuff the way the other two did,

Marie LeClaire

and nursed his drink slowly. He had a bad feeling and didn't want to lose his edge.

As the fire died down, so did James and Sarah, finishing off the jug. Propped up against a tree, James reached into his sack and pulled out his fiddle. As soon as he drew the first notes, Simeon jumped up. "What are you doing!? That thing will echo off the granite around here for miles. You might as well ring the church bell and let everyone know where we are."

"Aw, shut up about it. You act like you know everything." James yelled back in a drunken slur.

Sarah held up a hand. "They will not need the fiddle. They can hear you both howling at each other like sparring wildcats." Sarah's speech was slowed by the alcohol.

Simeon and James both calmed down.

"You know playing the fiddle eases my mind," James complained.

"I know," Simeon agreed. "Sorry. Just not tonight."

"Good enough." James lay the fiddle down beside his bedroll.

"I feel restless. I need to walk," Simeon stated.

"Sim, are you not noticing it is dark." Sarah stated the obvious.

"I know. I just need to move around a bit. I won't go far." And with that, he headed out of camp.

"He can be a real prissy-poo sometimes," James made a puckered face.

Sarah defended him. "I think sometimes he has a troubled soul."

Chapter 18

After ensuring the death of Abby and confirming instructions with the Guardian, John Morse left quickly out the back and headed to the river, to the Link. He traveled through the Links to Bridgewater and then to Salem, visited with an aunt there, then headed back to Fall River late in the day to resume his search for the Coin. He planned to claim that he left early in the day to visit family, the journey to Salem taking several hours. When he arrived back at the house, police and medical staff were everywhere. His niece, Lizzie, was sitting on the front lawn, eyes downward, still as a statue. In his thirst for revenge, it hadn't occurred to him that his niece would be the one to find them. What if she was harmed? He felt sick as he ran to comfort her. He ran up to the first officer he could find.

Feigning ignorance, he demanded, "What the devil is going on here?"

The officer stepped in front of him, barring his access to the grounds. "And who would you be?" he demanded back.

"John Morse. I'm Lizzie's uncle. I demand to know what has happened."

"Mr. and Mrs. Borden are dead, murdered inside the house. What do you know of that?"

Marie LeClaire

"What? Nothing at all. I left early this morning and am just now returning. Let me attend to Lizzie." He pushed past the officer and ran to Lizzie's side.

"Lizzie. Dear. Are you okay? What happened?"

Lizzie was barely alert. Staring at the ground, she began to rock. "They're dead. They think I did it."

John paled. This had gone terribly sideways. He needed to get that coin and get out of town. After reassuring himself that she was physically okay, he turned his attention to the house. He had searched the bedroom quickly after Abby's murder. The Coin was not to be found. Where was it? He needed to find that Coin. At the moment, there was no way he was getting into the house to continue his search. He waited impatiently with a nearly catatonic Lizzie while photos were taken and the bodies removed from the scene. As soon as the authorities cleared out, he resumed his search. The Legion would demand to know the whereabouts of both coins and if there was not a favorable answer, someone would be to blame. Finding the Coin would put him in a favorable light. The loss of it, not so much.

Lizzie was in the sitting room, in the chair her father had occupied earlier that day, staring into space. John grabbed her by the shoulders.

"Lizzie, dear. Are you listening? Where is your mother's jewelry? Her jewelry box is empty."

Lizzie looked vacantly at him, barely able to speak.

"Lizzie, talk to me. Do you know where your mother's jewelry is?" He shook her harder than he meant to.

She finally looked at him. "No. I don't know," she said meekly.

The Mistaken Haunting of Seth Harrison

John paced the floor as he had done just this morning. He had to find the Coin. Had Andrew taken it? No. If that were the case, the Guardian wouldn't have been able to attack him. It must be somewhere else. He headed out to the barn to see if the beast was still there.

He closed the barn door and took out his Coin. Holding it in his hand, he called out.

"Guardian. Come."

The beast appeared immediately.

"Did Andrew have his Coin this morning?"

The Guardian shook its head.

"Do you know where it is?"

The Guardian shook his head.

"The vagrants that were here this morning, could they have taken it?"

The Guardian remained still.

"Do you know where they are?"

The beast nodded.

"Take me to them."

Chapter 19

Simeon was at the edge of the cemetery grounds planning to walk the perimeter. The graveyard was shadowy in the moonlight and he could see the outline of the stones. He had to admit, it was a bit creepy. Suddenly the crystal gave him a jolt, like a needle going into his chest.

"Ooouuwww." He pulled it out from under his shirt and looked at it. It appeared to be glowing. At first, he assumed it was some kind of reflection of moonlight. But as he turned it over, the glow continued. He looked around. Two figures were walking quickly through the headstones. One looked like an average man in a long black overcoat and brimmed black hat. He looked familiar. Was he the man Simeon saw leaving the Borden house earlier this morning? The other looked like something out of old fairy tales, and not the good ones. This thing stood a full head taller than the man and wore a long black cape that dragged along the ground. An oversized hood hung low over its face. The cape fluttered in the breeze created by the swift pace they were keeping, partly revealing a body that appeared to be nothing but skin and bones underneath. This thing wore a sword attached to a belt around its waist that glinted when the moonlight hit it. They weren't using the cemetery paths but instead were walking straight toward the far edge of the grounds and the campsite, as if they knew it was there.

Marie LeClaire

The crystal glowed stronger as the two got closer. Simeon knew this wasn't good. He had just enough time to get to the camp before them. Heading off at the quietest run he could manage, he rushed into the clearing, kicking his two companions who were now in a dead sleep.

"Get up, get up," he whispered harshly.

"Huh, what?" James was barely moving.

Simeon didn't wait. He grabbed the carpet bag of cash and goods and leapt across the campsite, nudging Sarah on the way out.

"Sarah, get up. Run."

Sarah rolled over, drunkenly awake.

Terrified, Simeon kept going. He headed into the woods at a full run, clutching the bag close to his chest to keep it from rattling. After a few hundred feet, he realized he was not being followed. He looked back but saw no sign of the duo. He couldn't hear any footfalls either. He wondered if he had imagined the whole thing. He'd been a little jittery all day. As quietly as he could, he made his way back to the campsite. The embers of the fire were still glowing and the moon was high enough to shed some light into their little circle. He stood in horror as he watched the hooded figure striking Sarah repeatedly with a small axe. James reached for something to defend himself. He grabbed the first thing he could get his hands on, his fiddle, and raised it in defense. But it was useless. The figure pushed it aside and stuck James several times as well. James didn't even get out a scream. The man stood by silently.

"Search the bags," he commanded.

The creature grabbed Sarah's bag and emptied the contents onto the ground beside her body and sifted through its contents. Not finding what it was looking for, it

The Mistaken Haunting of Seth Harrison

emptied James' bag as well. Still empty handed, it stood to face the man.

"What do you mean it's not here? It has to be here, damn it!" the man growled. Simeon could hear panic rising in his voice.

The creature shook its head.

"Damn, where is it?" The man tossed through the contents on the ground in a panic. Then rifled through James' pockets. "It's not here!"

The creature held up a rotting hand. It had three fingers extended.

"There were three of them?"

A nod confirmed it.

"Where is the other one?"

The creature stood motionless.

"Do you know where the third beggar is?" he barked out.

The creature shook its head.

"Great!" The man looked around the site and into the darkened woods. "Blast! There's no point in searching in the dark. We could be here all night and not find him. For all we know, he ditched them hours ago. One thing's for sure, he has the Caller Coin."

Simeon stood, frozen, horrified, terrified. He held his breath as the man and the creature scanned the woods.

"We'll take the Link to Bridgewater. You guard the Link. I'll get a room at the inn and clean up." John looked down at his hands, covered with blood.

The thing nodded and waited. The man headed quickly into the woods away from Simeon. The beast fell into step close behind.

Simeon remained frozen. He could feel the crystal on his chest hot and vibrating. What should he do? Who were these two things? The broach Sarah stole must be the coin they were looking for. Why was it so important? Clearly, they were willing to kill for it - without any hesitation. And what kind of link would be further into the woods. Simeon needed to know what was going on. Silently, he followed the two into the darkness.

Within minutes, they emerged onto a well-worn path that appeared to head into town. Surprising Simeon, they turned in the opposite direction and picked up the pace.

"Hurry up, damn you. Time is essential. I will not let that Caller Coin go easily. As soon as the fuss dies down, we will resume our search for the third thief."

The creature nodded.

Simeon could hear clearly in the silence of the night as he crept out to the edge of the path. Stashing the bag out of sight along the edge of the trail, he continued to follow them. Where were these two going?

The trail opened up to a clearing along the river where there was a small dock. They walked up to the river's edge and stood, looking out. Directly in front of them, at the end of the dock, was a shimmering fog, oblong and about the height of an average man. It was like a window into some other place. His pendant gave a strong buzz. He pulled it out of his shirt. It was pulsing with energy. He looked back up to see the man and the creature step off the dock and into the hole. They didn't fall into the water or even hover above it. They literally walked through the hole and disappeared.

Simeon sat on the edge of the path for a long time, in shock, replaying the insane events of the night. What kind of hell had he stumbled upon? What should he do now? Poor Sarah and James. He couldn't get the images out of his head. At least they died quickly. But for what? What is

The Mistaken Haunting of Seth Harrison

this Caller Coin? One thing he knew for sure – he didn't want anything to do with it. Clearly this man and his beast would not stop looking for it. He had to get rid of it. Somewhere that they would find it. He'd go back to the house and leave it somewhere obvious. He had to hurry. He retrieved the bags and headed the other way along the path. It led him directly behind the factory belonging to Mr. Borden. He crept quietly around the side of the building, then slipped along the main street and into an alley.

The town was oddly busy considering most people should be just heading to bed. Something big had gone down and there were people everywhere. Creeping out of the alley, he saw the Borden house, a light in every room.

"What's going on?" he asked a spectator.

"There's been a murder," was the stunned reply. "There's never been a murder in Fall River."

"Who's that?" Simeon motioned to a slight figure, standing in front of the house, accompanied by a police officer.

"That's their daughter, Lizzie, poor thing. She's the one that found them."

"Them?"

"Yes, looks like Mr. and Mrs. Borden are both dead. Axed in their heads dozens of times is the gossip."

Simeon caught his breath. "Is that right?"

"Seems so," replied the man.

"She doesn't look very broken up about the situation." Simeon nodded to Lizzie.

"There's not many in town that will mourn the loss, truth be told."

Simeon's mind was racing. Had the same creature murdered this couple? Would they suspect he and his friends? That would put Simeon on the most wanted list for sure. He needed to get out of town, fast and far. But first he had to ditch this Caller Coin thing. Returning it to the house was out of the question. Dozens of people were coming and going. Quickly, he snuck around to the barn, slid in and closed the door behind him. Oddly, he didn't have the same foreboding as he did earlier. It just seemed like any other barn. He fumbled around in his bag until his hands got hold of the jewelry Sarah had taken. It must be this broach. His pendant gave him a little twinge as he grabbed it. "All the more reason to get rid of you," he said to it. He left it on one of the shelves figuring someone would find it soon enough. Then he high-tailed it out of town, heading for New Hampshire to find his sisters.

Present day

Chapter 20

Liam pulled the car into the parking lot of the Fall River Library. The three had taken a short walk around the waterfront park to clear their heads after the Coin heist.

Liam was hoping that the library's local transcripts and journals might have more information than what he received from Marilisa.

"So, any suggestions about how we proceed?" Liam needed Seth and Brit to buy into what he suspected was going to be the tedious process of research.

"Well, there are probably old newspapers from that day," Seth began.

"And court records maybe," Brit offered.

"Can we follow the ownership of the house? That might give us motive or at least a line to the next of kin," Seth added.

"You guys are on a roll," Liam replied. "We know someone in the family, and likely in the house, possessed a Caller Coin. It doesn't mean there was a Guardian around but due to the brutality of the crimes, most likely that was true. So, we're also looking for any other unusual things or events."

"Do you really think it was a Guardian?"

"Considering what we know now, I hardly think Lizzie capable of it."

"I don't know," Brit took the opposing view. "By reports, they were both mean to Lizzie and her sister. Being abused by the man her whole life has to be considered. There are many days when I think about it."

"Thinking about it and doing it are two very different things," Liam cautioned her.

"Everyone has a breaking point."

"Well, let's see where the evidence leads us. Brit, you work on the assumption that Lizzie reached that breaking point and ended the abuse by ending the lives of her abusers. Seth, you follow the lead of some outside source setting the stage for Lizzie to take the fall."

"Okay, that sounds fun," Brit was ready to go.

"You're on," Seth challenged Brit. "And to the winner?" He directed his question at Liam.

"Dinner and a movie selected by the winner."

"Done," Seth agreed.

"Done," Brit nodded.

The Fall River Public Library was well appointed, with computer terminals for public use and a digitized catalog system. Modern furniture gave it a café style décor. These modern conveniences were not for them, as it turns out. They wound their way around to the old microfiche rolls, where large viewing stations that looked like the old analog TV sets had hand cranks and manual loading trays.

The Mistaken Haunting of Seth Harrison

They pulled out newspaper scrolls running from four weeks before the murders to four weeks after. Seth was tasked with reviewing police blotters and legal notices. Brit was to read everything she could find about the investigation. Liam would review property plats and old deeds in a room even further back. He could also review the historical tax records, researching the family wealth. Seth and Brit were happy to get some alone time sitting side by side at the microfiche machines.

"I'm sure Lizzie did it," she baited Seth.

"There's no way. Look at her." He pointed to a photo on Brit's screen. "She's all skinny and barely 5 feet tall. How's she going to overpower her father?"

"Ah, he was *asleep*. Weren't you listening?"

"Maybe, maybe not. And there was that uncle who was supposedly there but then not. That sounds pretty unusual, doesn't it?" Seth asked.

"I'll give you that," she conceded. "But he didn't have motive."

"That we know of, yet."

"Well, let's get to it, then."

They both turned to their respective screens, happy to be working together.

After an hour of squinting at the screens, they'd come up with next to nothing.

"Remind me why I never want to be a researcher," Brit rubbed her eyes. "An hour of this and I haven't found anything useful except maybe this article about the uncle who was supposedly there that day." She sat back in her chair. "I'm hungry."

"Me too, just one more page and I'm done with this spool." Seth turned one more page to the police blotter which was always in the back of the edition. "OH MY

Marie LeClaire

GOD!" Seth's eyes got really big. His breathing stopped. He was frozen, glued to the screen.

"What!? What?!" Brit rolled her chair over to view his screen. "Oooohhhhhhhhhh." She too became glued to the screen. Before them, backlit in the antique viewer, was a photo of the ghosts that were haunting Seth. Brit pushed a frozen Seth out of the way and read the article out loud.

"Two bodies were found behind the Oak Grove Cemetery late yesterday afternoon. Authorities estimate they have been dead for several weeks. They were identified with assistance by law enforcement in Bridgewater and Brockton as James Smith and Sarah McDougal, grifters that were working their way south from Boston. According to local merchants, they came through town a few weeks ago with another man believed to be Simeon Harrison. He is suspected in their deaths which were of a very brutal nature, each victim stabbed several times. A love triangle is the assumed motive."

The photo was of their decomposing bodies but the connection was unmistakable. James and Sarah were the ghosts haunting Seth, down to the clothes and hair.

Seth and Brit were still seated together, staring at the backlit microfiche when Liam came by to spring them for lunch.

"How did you make out?" He came around to look at the screen. "Oh." Liam immediately recognized the ghosts in the newspaper article. "Well, isn't that interesting?"

Brit was the first to take a breath. "It's Seth's ghosts."

"Yes, it is." Liam leaned in to read. "What's the story."

"It looks like Simeon Harrison killed them," Brit reported.

The Mistaken Haunting of Seth Harrison

Seth came out of his shock. "That's what they meant by HE KILLED US. Not me, him." Seth pointed at the screen. "Simeon Harrison."

"Same name," Liam pointed out. "Maybe it's a relative. It's believed that ghosts can move on once they've accomplished or completed some task in our world, like justice or amends for something they did. If the ghosts believe you are a relative of their murderer, that would explain the hauntings."

"If it is, he didn't do it," Seth felt the need to defend this alleged ancestor.

"That's a very loyal stance, Seth. Back it up. What are the facts?"

Seth spun around on his chair. "First of all, no one saw him do it."

"Okay, anything else?" Liam prompted.

"Well, no, not yet."

"Here's something," Brit added. "This newspaper is from four weeks after the Borden murders, but the murders themselves happened weeks before their bodies were found, according to the article. That means that both murders could have happened around the same time. And the murders are remarkably similar. So, if Lizzie committed the Borden murders, then why would she kill these other two, assuming the same killer?"

Seth's brain started kicking in. "And if Simeon was the murderer, why would he kill the Bordens? He would have hardly known them."

"And if it was a Guardian," Liam added, "why would he kill all four of them? Guardians only kill on the command of a handler. Either by a cleric, or a Caller Coin holder, or perhaps someone with some other powerful magic."

Marie LeClaire

"Like what?" Seth wondered what other kinds of magic there were out there to be concerned about.

"There is a rumor about higher levels of magic but no one knows for sure. At least not the people I've ever talked to."

Brit picked up on Liam's comment. "What do you mean, no one you have ever talked to? How many people know about this stuff?"

"More than you would think, both here in the US and all over Europe and Asia. Links are found all over the world. It's believed that if such magic still exists, it's likely hidden in Europe with roots in Celtic tradition."

"My head hurts." Seth leaned over and ran his fingers through his hair.

"Yes, it's time to eat and get some fresh air. Let's take a break, which is why I came over here in the first place." They printed out the two articles related to the second murders, then returned the rolls to the shelves before heading out.

They settled in for lunch at a pizza place across the street. Seth and Brit shared their findings from the old newspapers. Aside from Seth's ghost story, not much was new. Brit complained about the shoddy investigation that followed the Borden murders, which was unable to conclusively corroborate her *Lizzie did it* platform.

"I found something like what you were talking about, Liam," Brit said as she stretched the cheese off the last piece of pizza. "The maid said she saw John Morse that morning for breakfast but friends in Salem claim he was there around the same time. Two places at once."

"Good job. Both of you." Liam was looking over a copy of the article on James and Sarah. "It says here that they were buried in the pauper's grave at Oak Grove

Cemetery. What do you say we go there this afternoon and see what we can find?"

"Sure," Brit was excited. The more morbid the better in her book.

Seth was not so excited. "There's probably nothing there anymore. It's been a hundred years."

"Believe me, it's there," Liam replied. "If there's one thing that stands the test of time, it's cemeteries. No one wants to wake the dead. So, unless there's a really good reason to move them, they remain untouched for hundreds of years. They last longer than any building, no matter how historic."

"Okay, let's go," Seth gave in. "At least we'll be outside."

Chapter 21

They came out of the Oak Grove Cemetery office with a map of Pauper's Field.

"I had no idea cemeteries had offices that you could ask to find someone's grave." Brit was amazed.

"Sometimes they even have the obituaries on file. Due to James' and Sarah's indigent status, there wasn't a lot of fuss made for their burial but we should at least be able to find their markers and maybe get an idea of where they were murdered."

"Two murder sites in one day! Will it get any better?" Brit was elated.

"Be careful what you ask for," Liam cautioned.

"Yeah, seriously," Seth was getting grumpier by the minute.

They walked past the large Borden plot with a small iron fence surrounding it. The towering monument in the center listed several family members including Andrew and Abby. Lizzie's name appeared at the bottom of the list.

In the far back corner of the property, they came to the Pauper's Plot. It was a large area bounded on all sides by a service road, as if to prevent the poor from mingling with the rest of the residents. There were no upright stones, each grave marked by a well-weathered plaque flush with the ground.

"Let's see," Liam pulled out the map from the office. According to this, the graves are side by side, four rows up and ten in from this side."

"One, two, three," Brit started counting off.

"It's right here. This must be it." Seth called from up ahead. He was bent over, pulling grass off an old slab of granite.

"Really?" Brit ran to see. "Wow. Just like they said." Seth and Brit were looking down at two small stone markers that had sunk appreciably into the ground. "JS and SM, D 1892. No date of birth. I guess they didn't have that."

"It's not like today when we all carry IDs with personal information. I'm surprised they knew their names at all," Liam pointed out.

"Can we go now. There's nothing else here." Seth was wringing his hands and looking around.

"Are you okay, Seth?" Liam was more curious than concerned.

"No. I don't like it here."

"Alright. Why don't we take the long way out, walking up over the knoll where the bodies were found? It's all been cleared now to extend the cemetery but the general area is back this way."

Seth couldn't come up with a good reason not to and he couldn't let himself be outdone by Brit, but he was feeling really nervous all of a sudden. He put his hand to his chest where the crystal laid against his skin. He didn't like this.

They circled around the base of the knoll which brought them in view of the river a few hundred yards away. It was late afternoon and the sun was closing in on the horizon, casting an orange hue into the air.

"Ouch." Seth grabbed at his chest.

"Seth, what's going on?" Liam insisted.

"It's my mother's pendent. It's acting all weird. It just sort of stabbed me."

"What do you mean 'your mother's'?"

"I got it when I was discharged. It was in an old box of my things that the police had."

"Has it ever done that before?"

"A few times before but I never paid any attention because... you know, hallucinations?"

Liam sighed. "Yes, I understand. Tell me what's happening now."

"Well, before, when we found the Caller Coin it was kind of humming. I don't know how to describe it but it's uncomfortable, like nerves or something."

"When did it start again? Just now?"

"It's been getting worse since we got to the graves, and just now it like kicked me."

"Okay, Seth. I'm going to ask you to touch it and see if you can make it worse."

"What? Are you crazy?"

"It might be trying to alert you to something." Liam's patience was waning.

"Well, I don't think I want to know what it is."

"Come on, Seth." It was Brit adding to the conversation. "We've come this far."

"Alright." He laid an hand on the pendent under his shirt, took a deep breath and turned slowly in all directions. "It's definitely worse this way." He pointed toward the river.

"Let's go." Liam started to walk in that direction.

"What! Why?" Seth was frozen.

Marie LeClaire

Liam turned around with a huff. "The pendent isn't trying to kill you. It's trying to tell you something. Let's go."

Seth looked to Brit for support.

Brit shrugged. "Are you feeling bad or just weird?"

Seth thought for a moment. "Just weird I guess."

"Then maybe we should check it out. It might be some kind of message from your mother."

"Yeah. Maybe." Seth started walking slowly toward the river. He felt more and more uncomfortable until he finally pulled the crystal out of his shirt. It was glowing.

Liam was excited. "Has it ever done that before?"

"Not that I know of. I've only had it a few weeks."

"Hold it up."

Seth did as he was told. It cast a faint light out toward the river.

"This way," Liam commanded heading in the direction of the light.

He stopped them about fifteen feet away from the river's edge, then indicated that Seth should move forward. Tentatively Seth took a few steps. A shimmer appeared. Liam coaxed him on silently. Seth stepped closer. The shimmer intensified. He quickly stepped back again.

"Have you seen anything like this before?" Liam asked quietly, looking around to see if they were being noticed.

"Yes. But I've never gotten this close. I used to go the other way, you know, hallucin...."

Liam interrupted him. "Yes, yes. I get it."

Liam turned to Brit.

"Yes, I've seen it too, I think, at the hospital. I never got close either. It's a little creepy."

"Seth, take another step."

"Really Doc? Are you sure it won't hurt me?"

"I'm sure...mostly."

"Great." Seth took another step then another. The shimmer glowed stronger and grew larger till it was almost seven feet across and oval.

"One more step," Liam coached.

As Seth took the step, the shimmer changed and a hole began opening up in the middle. It continued getting larger, until a view could be seen, like a window to somewhere else. Seth stared at the Link with huge eyes, hardly breathing. There was still a thick haze on the image making it unclear where it went.

"Step back," Liam ordered.

Gratefully, Seth did as he was told, letting out his breath as he did so. Brit took a few steps in to grab his arm and pull him back a few more steps. She stood close to him as they both turned to Liam.

"What the hell is that?" Seth whispered.

"That....is a Link."

Chapter 22

Liam's heart was pumping with adrenalin. Seth had spotted the Link easily and it had responded to him instantly. The crystal seemed to act as a magic finder of sorts.

"Where does it go?" Brit was whispering.

"That's the question, isn't it? We'll have to go through to find out."

"Seriously???" They were both looking at him with disbelief, their eyes nearly popping out of their heads.

Liam's excitement was turning to irritation. "Yes, seriously." He stared them both down with an *I mean business* glare. "But there's an immediate problem. Did you notice the haze that it has on the image in the center?" Liam approached the Link and reached out his hand, attempting to push it through. The surface waved slightly like water at his touch but did not yield.

"Just as I thought." Liam paused to consider this.

"What!" barked Seth. "Why do you do that?"

"Do what?" Liam asked distractedly.

"Half say something!"

Liam turned to him calmly. "The last time I offered unsolicited advice, you ran away from home."

"Well, okay." Seth calmed down. "There's that. But I'm not doing that now. So, WHAT already?"

"The Link appears to be locked."

Marie LeClaire

Brit jumped in to keep the peace. "What does that mean, exactly?"

"No one can pass through until a Link Opener releases it. I'm guessing that's where you come in, Seth."

"Me? What do I do? I don't know anything about this stuff." Seth took a step back.

"If you're an Opener, it should just come naturally to you. All I know is that it involves moving hands in a certain way. So, just try something."

Seth fussed with his hands for a moment. "This is stupid. I have no idea what I'm doing."

Liam was almost badgering him now. "Just step up to the Link and do whatever comes to you."

"You can do it," Brit was more encouraging. "If you were making it up, what would it be?"

Seth reluctantly stepped up to the Link, close enough to see the hazy center image of the other side. He reached out to touch the Link. He felt a pushback from the shimmer field. It wasn't painful, just a resistance. "This is stupid. I don't know what to do." He was getting frustrated already.

"Wave your hand in a clockwise circle." Liam directed. He was hoping that if he could get Seth moving, intuition would take over.

Seth waved his left hand clockwise, palm parallel with the Link, one full circle. The Link shimmered a bit brighter.

"Change it up in some way, like making it bigger or make two circles or something else." Liam continued to coax him.

Seth stood up a little taller, held his hand out in front and made one small circle. A bright spot started at the center of the image, like a sparkler at a 4th of July

The Mistaken Haunting of Seth Harrison

celebration. When Seth stopped, the sparkle stopped. Seth waved again. The sparkle slowly grew outward then stopped. They were all mesmerized, watching Seth manipulate the link. Seth continued to wave in circles and the sparkle worked out from the center, as if burning away a veil, until it reached the edges of the shimmer. They all stood there, amazed. As much as Liam bragged about his knowledge, his actual field experience fell seriously short of his presentation. He had certainly never seen anyone open a Link before and he had only passed through one once. The air around them instantly changed, as if the Link had let in a breeze from the other side. Instinctively, they all turned around to make sure they were still alone. They all looked at each other, then back at the Link. Through the window they could see what appeared to be a field or meadow butting up against a wooded area about twenty feet away. The image was tunnel-like and no amount of peering around the edges would show them the area to the sides.

"What happens now?" Seth turned to Liam.

"We go through. But there's one more thing I need to tell you before we do."

"Yeah?" Seth was expecting some last minute *it might hurt a little* information. He was not prepared for what came next.

Liam took a deep breath. "There are sometimes Guardians on the other side of the Link. Sometimes you can see them, sometimes you can't."

"And?"

"And it's their job to make sure no one passes through the Link."

Brit was wondering what else Liam wasn't telling them. "Well, if we can't see them, how do we know if they're there?"

"We don't. We go through and if they are there, we come immediately back through to this side."

"Or what?" Brit kept at it.

"Or they might kill us."

"WHHAAATTT????!!!" they both screamed.

Waving his arms desperately, Liam tried to quiet them. "SHHHHHH, SSSHHHHH. Be quiet."

They weren't exactly calming down, but at least the volume went back to a whisper. They stood staring at him.

"Kill us?" Seth insisted. "When were you going to tell us about this?"

"Now. Now was when. It didn't seem important if we couldn't get through the Link."

"Why did you think we couldn't?" Brit asked.

"I knew it was locked. Links can only be opened by an Opener and they are all assumed dead."

"But you told me I could do it. How did you know?"

"I didn't. But there's something unique about you. Call it a hunch."

"What are we going to do now?" Brit asked.

"The Guardians don't think independently. They don't set a trap but they hide out of sight of any humans so as not to draw attention. They are usually ordered to prevent anyone from using the Link but not necessarily to kill them. Again, not to draw attention. So, if there is a Guardian, he's hiding close enough for us to see him when we get through the Link. Because this link has been closed, I suspect there is no one guarding it."

"Maybe we shouldn't go through. Really, what's the point?" Surprisingly, it was Brit who was backtracking now.

"It might give us some insight into why Seth is being haunted?" Liam offered. He knew it was thin and he was counting on their curiosity to move this forward.

"Okay, let's do it. Do we just walk straight through?" Seth walked up to the Link.

"Wait. Let's all go through together." Liam and Brit walked up beside him, with Brit positioning herself between the two. They could now see the landscape on the other side. There was no Guardian as far as they could see.

"It won't hurt but watch your footing on the other side. Sometimes it knocks you a little off balance." Liam sounded much more confident than he was. "Ready?" he asked.

Brit took Seth's hand. "Ready."

Seth nodded and they stepped through the Link.

Chapter 23

Liam, Seth and Brit stepped out at the tree line of dense woods. They quickly looked around for any danger that might be lurking nearby. All seemed clear. Taking another few steps forward, they heard a slight crackling sound behind them. They turned to see the Link, with a line of sparkles moving from the edges to the center, as it faded back to a faint shimmering fog, this time with a clear image of the riverbank on the other side. As they backed away, the Link faded more, taking on a light foggy appearance. Almost more startling than the Link was the view behind it. Slicing between the earth and sky were the large grey walls of Bridgewater State Hospital. Off to the left, Seth noticed the outbuilding that acted as home for forty-five clinically crazy adolescents. He wondered for a moment if there were others like him in there.

"This is messed up," Seth was the first to speak. "Is there anyone else like me in there?" He gave a nod to the adolescent unit.

"Not that I'm aware of. I haven't been back since you were discharged."

Seth turned to the prison. "What about there?"

"Not that I know of. But one of the guards has a Caller Coin."

"Seriously?" they said in unison.

Marie LeClaire

"Yes. I'm not sure if he knows what it is. He referred to it as his good luck charm. Now that I think about it, his name is Borden."

"What!" Brit's eyes widened. "Back then the Borden's owned half the town, maybe more. If they all had Caller Coins, they must have known about the Links. How far is Salem from here? That's where John Morse was seen."

"Too far to travel in our time frame," Liam explained.

"But there's another Link on the other side of the property." Seth's statement stunned them all for a moment.

They were interrupted when dogs started to bark from inside the fence.

"Well, we know where this goes, so I say we head back to the cemetery. And quickly, before we get noticed." Liam stepped toward the link which did the sparkly thing in reverse, from the center outward.

"I vote for that," Brit seconded.

"Me too," Seth grabbed Brit's hand and joined Liam as they passed through the Link together.

The sun was approaching the horizon as they stepped back through the Link onto the river bank. They looked around quickly. Liam noticed Seth was holding onto Brit's hand.

Seth and Brit realized it too, and awkwardly let go.

"Okay, that was really weird," Brit took a deep breath.

"Yeah, I'm not sure how I feel about it." Seth physically shook off the experience.

"Keep alert," Liam warned. He looked around as they headed back into the cemetery. Seth and Brit following along.

The Mistaken Haunting of Seth Harrison

They were coming down the knoll at the edge of the manicured grounds when Liam noticed a vapor tentacle rising from behind a headstone in front of them.

"Heads up. There," he nodded the direction. While the first vapor was taking form, several others started rising to the sky, joined by more. Forming behind the gravestones were ghosts of all shapes and sizes. All standing very still, looking at the visitors. Some with curiosity, some looked fearful. The ones in the front had taken on a more adversarial stance, eyes thin, arms crossed. The one closest to them floated out from behind the headstone. He was a large round man with a hole in his chest. His clothes were more likely from the Middle Ages than from any era in North America.

"That Link's been locked for over a hundred years," he eyed them suspiciously. "You a Link Opener?" the ghost asked.

Liam was shocked to hear a ghost talking to him.

Seth whispered "You said they couldn't talk to us?"

"Apparently they can," he whispered back.

"We can hear too," the ghost growled. "Are you a Link Opener?" he insisted.

Liam hesitated, not wanting to give up Seth. "Yes."

"You're a liar," the ghost growled. Several of the closest ghosts floated slightly forward.

"Not me. The lad here." Liam pointed toward Seth.

"That, I believe." The other ghosts backed off again.

"My name is Liam."

"They call me Sour Puss. I run things around here."

"It was my understanding that ghosts and humans can't communicate easily."

"When you get to be my age, it gets easier."

"And how old is that?" asked Brit innocently.

"Didn't your mother teach you manners? It's not polite to ask an old person how old they are."

"Oh, I'm sorry. No offense intended." Brit took a step back, and a little behind Seth who took a protective step forward.

Sour Puss lightened his tone. "Aawwhh, I don't really care anyway. Maybe because I don't remember how old I am. Older than everyone else here. That's for sure." His voice still had a gravelly bark to it. "And what's your name?" He nodded at Seth.

"Seth. Seth Harrison."

"Really?" Puss's attitude turned curious. He leaned in toward Seth. He had the same name as James and Sarah's friend. Three came through, one got out alive.

"How old are ye?"

"18," Seth almost stuttered.

"Really? Hmmm."

"Who's this?" Puss nodded toward Brit but continued to look at Seth.

"My friend, Brit."

Brit nodded agreement.

"Are you with the Consortium or the Legion?"

Seth wondered for a split second if there was a right answer. "I don't know. Neither I guess."

"If I could be helpful here," Liam stepped in. "We are not working for either organization but our friendship would be more to the Consortium."

Puss looked Liam over for a moment. Turning to the other ghosts, he gave them the slightest nod, and one by one they vaped back to wherever they had come from.

"What brings you here?" This question was directed at Liam.

The Mistaken Haunting of Seth Harrison

"Seth has been haunted by a couple of young ghosts and we are trying to find out why."

"I'm sure I don't know." Puss replied.

"If there are no answers for us here, we'll be going. Would you like us to close the Link?"

"No. We're glad to have it open again. It makes things easier for us."

"No problem." Liam looked over to Seth and Brit, nodded in the direction of the car and started walking.

Puss called after them, "Be careful using these Links. Some of them are trouble."

They were safely back in the car when Liam broke the silence. "Everyone alright?"

"I don't know if I'd say that, exactly, but I'm not hurt." Seth patted down his body.

Brit was still a little breathless. "Yeah, not hurt."

"Okay. So. That was your welcome to the other world," Liam explained. "The one most people don't even know exists."

"How can they not know?" Seth demanded.

"You of all people should know that, Seth. We have doctors that tell us what is possible and what is not. We diagnose and medicate anything that falls outside of a very small circle. And honestly, most people choose not to know. Life is simpler that way."

"I'm starting to see the appeal in that." Seth was slumped over in the back seat.

"Maybe. But it's hard to unknow now," Brit insisted.

"I see that too. I feel like there's no going back," Seth moaned.

"Well, I for one have no desire to go back, Seth Harrison." Brit turned and leaned over the seat to look him

Marie LeClaire

square in the face. "You don't understand. These last few days have validated my entire life! The last few years anyway. I'm excited to know all these amazing things exist." She was on a roll. "I'm not going back to my other life."

"I'm afraid you'll have to," Liam said.

"What!?" She snapped her head around to the front seat.

"Brit, look. First of all, you're a minor. Granted a 17-year-old very mature minor but by law a minor nonetheless. You have to go back to the foster home, finish high school and maybe even go to college."

"No, I don't!"

"Yes, you do." Surprisingly, this came from Seth.

"What?!"

Seth continued, "If you don't go home or don't go to school, it's going to draw attention, and not the good kind. If it makes you feel any better, I still have to go to my crummy job and earn money. The ghosts aren't going to pay the rent or buy groceries."

"I guess." Brit felt defeated.

"We'll include you in whatever we do, but we still have to do other stuff too. Right Liam?" He didn't sound as confident as he wanted to.

"Absolutely. Even I have a regular job."

"Okay," Brit relented. "But that was totally freaking cool."

"Yeah," Seth grinned, "It kinda was."

Chapter 24

Puss watched as the three walked to their car. They were no sooner out of the parking lot, when the dearly departed started popping up everywhere. Ghosts of all shapes and sizes were whispering, giggling, and floating back and forth to each other. Puss studied them all with a grumpy face. Finally, a young Revolutionary War soldier approached him.

"Hey, Puss. Is it true? Did that kid open up the old Link?

"True, Daniel."

"What do you think? Is it safe?"

"Could be, or not. I'm not too trusting of neither the Legion nor the Consortium at the moment. Better settle everyone down while I check it out."

"Yes, sir, Mr. Puss." Daniel snapped to attention with a salute.

"Quit that, Daniel! I told you I ain't your commanding officer."

"Right, Mr. Puss, sir." Daniel relaxed a little. "I'll do my best, but they're already itching to get through it."

"They've waited for a hundred years, most of them. They can wait a little while longer." Puss waved him off.

Puss recalled the day the Link had been closed by Charles Borden, Andrew's cousin and an Opener, the day after the bodies were discovered. A Guardian remained in

Marie LeClaire

the cemetery for a few weeks even though the Link was closed. Puss figured he was waiting to see if anyone came sniffing around either to the campsite or the Link. Puss couldn't be sure, but he suspected it was Andrew's Guardian.

When Andrew was alive, he allowed them to use the Link as long as they didn't get in the way of his business. During the War Between the States, Charles Borden owned B & B Ironworks in Bridgewater which was manufacturing guns for the Union Army. Charles and Andrew were redirecting a portion of the product to be sold to the Confederates where they could get triple the price. Charles would sneak the goods out of the factory in Bridgewater, pass them through the Link to Andrew at the Taunton River Link that passed by the cemetery's rear border and load them on small cargo ships. From there the transports would hug the coast down to Norfolk, Virginia, where the cargo was sold and other legitimate cargo, like cotton, was loaded and shipped back to the Borden mill in Fall River. After the war, the process reversed itself when goods were sent to rebuild the south while the northern-bound ships carried illegally confiscated spoils of war.

In any case, it was live and let live for the dearly departed. They didn't care much about his business as long as the Link was available to them. They gave the Guardian a wide berth but the situation was volatile and the possibility for things getting out of hand was always present.

Sour Puss turned to the gathered departed. "You all stay put while I see what's on the other side of this thing," he hollered at them. He floated to the back of the cemetery and hovered over the water for a moment, staring through the misty doorway to what used to be the old farm at

Bridgewater State Hospital. He had a couple of vaper friends on the other side, near the asylum, that he used to visit regularly. He didn't get a chance to talk to them much anymore but they had told him it was a prison for crazy people now. So, he wasn't sure what to expect.

As soon as he stepped through the Link, he saw two departed souls off in the distance headed in his direction at high speed. He hesitated, waiting to see who they were.

"Well, kill me twice! If it isn't the honorable Sir Sour Puss," came the squeal of a lovely lady ghost headed straight for him. She vaporized just before impact, running a ribbon of smoke around his translucence.

"Ha ha ha, Isabella! Aren't you a sight for sore eyes?" Puss's grin went from ear to ear and then some, distorting the lower part of his face like a cartoon.

The vaper streamed straight up to the sky and then swooped down to reform at his side. Isabella was a lovely woman from the colonial gentry of Boston. A woman of breeding, she also had a heart for adventure which is what got her killed one night down by the docks. Puss loved the bad girl/nobility combination.

"You are as beautiful as the day you died, my dear."

"Oh, you say the nicest things." She tilted her head downward in false modesty.

"Evening, Puss," came a greeting from behind Isabella. Christian Mathers floated out into view. "We heard the Link was open. Had to come see if it was true."

"It sure is. I saw the Link Opener myself."

"One of those evil Borden brothers, was it?"

"You would have thought that, or one of their kin, but no. It was a youngster. He looked a bit startled by the whole thing, if you ask me." Puss was smiling and shaking his head. "Clearly a novice. You should have seen the look

Marie LeClaire

on his face." Puss made his eyes bulge out disturbingly far from their sockets. They all let out a ghostly howl.

"Seriously though," Christian continued, "What do you think is going on?"

"I can't tell yet. The boy is certainly new to his powers, and a strong one at that, but his mentor feels a little shifty to me. His name's Liam. You ever heard of him?"

"Oh yeah, we know him," Christian and Isabella were both nodding their heads. "He comes around here from time to time, snooping if you ask me."

Isabella added, "I don't like him much either although there's no reason not to. He's never done anything cross."

"Tonight either. It's just something about him." Puss stroked his vapor beard.

"Are they going to leave the Link open?" There was a little excitement in Isabella's voice.

"I'm not sure. For the time being it looks that way. I don't think they have any plans for it exactly, at least not yet."

"Will we be seeing more of you then?" Christian asked. "I understand you're not getting out much."

"I'm not so inclined to travel like I used to and truth be told, things at the cemetery keep me pretty busy. There's over a hundred departed just in the cemetery alone now, and another fifty in town. The personalities and politics are wearing me out."

"We're lucky to have you in leadership, Puss. You know we all look to you for guidance." Christian commented.

"Well, maybe not all," Puss corrected him.

"What do you mean," Isabella was surprised. "Are there factions out your way? Descension?"

The Mistaken Haunting of Seth Harrison

"The new ones think they know how to do things better. They're not so interested in hearing from the elders. You know how it goes. I'm sure it will die down in a few years. We all seem to have a lot of time. Speaking of which, I thought you moved on, Isabella."

"I could have after I made things right with my great granddaughter but I'm just not ready to go yet. I'm pretty sure I can move on any time I want now, I'm just choosing to stay."

"Well, I'm glad to see you. You can come through my Link any time you want." Puss gave her a wink and a nod.

"I surely will, sir." She gave him a curtsey.

"And Christian, don't be a stranger. Let's keep an eye on things and if you get any information or something changes on your side, come right on over and let me know."

"We sure will. Do you think it's safe to start using it again?"

"I can't see any reason why not. It's safe on the cemetery end, for the time being anyway."

"Surely, then. Give our regards to the others." Christian waved a vapory hand.

"I will. Good day now." And with that, Puss passed back through the Link to the cemetery.

Chapter 25

Deep in the heart of the King's Legion headquarters, Grand Knight Malik Grundeldon was pacing slowly back and forth across the stone floor of his chambers. Despite the summer warmth, the old Spencer Abbey always felt cold and damp. He could have found offices in a more conventional place, but he liked the abbey for its atmosphere, its history, its solitude – and its Link.

"There have been changes recently, Mildred, and I'm not sure I like it." He paused in front of his desk. "Someone has opened the Oak Grove Link." Malik stared off into space as he ran his hand down Mildred's back and along her tail. "Do you think it's the boy? We wiped out those family lines generations ago."

Mildred purred loudly, "*Mmmrrrwww.*"

Malik turned his glare on her. "Are you suggesting that the Legion did not complete that task?"

"*Mrrrwwooooeww.*"

"Yes. You could be right. It's hard to know exactly what happened a hundred years ago. The boy does seem to be unusual. Even still, the Borden line has continued since then and there's been no Openers among them since Charles' death."

After slaughtering all known Openers and their families, the Legion gained control over the US Link network through Charles Borden, the country's last

Marie LeClaire

Opener and a staunch member of the King's Legion. Charles was ordered to close many of the Links, opening them only as needed. No one had foreseen his untimely death in a freak factory accident. High Command had frantically poured through historical documents looking for lost blood lines, without success.

"Mmmeeeerrrrooow. Hsss."

"Of course, it was short sighted. But those times were much more chaotic. Links were open all over the place. Unsuspecting imbeciles were falling through them all the time, getting murdered by unsupervised Guardians."

Mildred jumped to the floor. "*Mmmmeeeoooooow?*"

"Yes, please continue to stay with McMurty. I need some eyes on the situation there until I'm clear on where his allegiance lies."

Mildred looked up at him then turned her tail end to him in response.

"I know you don't like it there but you admitted it's gotten better since the young ones arrived. I simply must keep a close eye on this situation. I'll make it up to you."

As Mildred was heading out, Malik called through the open door.

"Cameron! Get in here."

Cameron reported on the run. "Yes, Sir Malik. How can I be of service to the Legion?"

"The Oak Grove Link has been opened."

Cameron hid his surprise, remaining at attention. "Yes sir."

"I want you to go there and see what's happening."

"Yes sir. Do you know who opened it sir?"

"If I did, why would I be sending you!"

"Yes sir. My apologies Commander." Cameron backed up bowing low.

"I'll bet you McMurty has something to do with it," Malik grumbled. "He's been sniffing around Fall River with two teenagers."

"Yes, sir. Do you want me to kill them?" Cameron stood upright again.

"No! What I want is for you to stop trying to think and just do as you're told."

"Yes, sir."

"Go to the cemetery first thing tomorrow. See if Puss is talking. Find out what you can."

"Yes sir."

"Very well."

"Should I post a Guardian there?"

"Not yet. No sense getting the whole cemetery in a stir."

"Yes sir."

"That is all."

Mildred, who was hanging around in the outer room getting a very satisfying scratch from the guard, turned her nose up as Cameron walked by. The guard leaned closer to Mildred and whispered, "I know what you mean."

As soon as the threesome were safely back at home, Liam stepped out to the patio to check in with the Counsel. After all, they were paying him.

"Hello Liam," Fay had her usual standoffish tone, always on guard against Liam bringing up the subject of his father.

Liam was sarcastically sweet in response. "Hello Fay."

"Are you whispering?"

Marie LeClaire

"The young people are in the house. I'm just trying for a little privacy. Unless you don't think it's necessary?"

"Yes. Of course. Discretion, by all means. What have you found?"

"I've found a Link in Fall River." He suspected she already knew.

"Very good, Liam. Please send me the information."

"Don't you want to know if it's open?" He suspected she knew this too.

"Yes. Of course. Is it?"

"Yes." Liam needed this to go his way. "I'd like to deliver the information directly to the counsel, if I may. In person. I have maps and a theory about its past use by the Legion." He wanted to corner the Counsel for information by withholding his findings. He knew they knew more than they were saying.

Fay hesitated. "I'm not sure that can happen in a timely way, Liam. Best just send the information electronically and I'll get back to you on it."

"Yes. Of course. I'll get right on it."

Fay hung up the phone and turned to Marilisa. "Contact the counsel. We need to meet in Fall River. Tell them to make immediate plans and wait for my word."

"Do you think he's got information he's not sharing? Maybe it has to do with the boy."

"How would I know what he's not saying." Fay dodged Marilisa's not-so-subtle fishing for information.

"Just saying. He sounds like he has an agenda."

"We all have an agenda, don't we, Marilisa? Besides, Mildred is keeping us apprised of the situation.

Chapter 26

Liam looked up from the dining room table to see James and Sarah on the patio. As he stepped out the door, James and Sarah skittered backward.

"Well, I guess you're here to see Seth."

The ghosts nodded slowly. James was trying for as sinister a face as he could make, with squinty eyes and pursed lips.

"We were just reading about you in the paper today."

Sarah raised her eyebrows. James stood fast.

"Oh, we were at the library in Fall River, reading old newspapers about your death."

They stared at him.

"We think maybe Simeon didn't do it."

James stamped his foot silently, putting his hands on his hips. Sarah turned to James and started jabbering on about it. Liam couldn't hear anything but he was pretty sure it started with *See, I told you so*. He suppressed a grin.

"If you promise not to kill Seth, you can come in and talk about it." Liam knew there was no serious risk, but he wanted some commitment for a calm discussion. All a person had to do was take a swipe at the ghost's vaporous body and they could do some damage. It wouldn't kill them but it would slow them down considerably.

James shook his head no.

"Okay, can you agree to hear us out before you try to kill Seth?"

James hesitated until Sarah yelled something at him. He nodded reluctantly.

James started miming something. He pointed at Liam, grabbed his own neck and pretended to choke himself with an exaggerated eye-bulging face, then released himself and pointed at Liam shaking his head aggressively.

"Ah, you want to know if I'm going to hurt you?"

James nodded.

"No. I have no intention of hurting you or Sarah."

They looked surprised, then suspicious, when Liam used her name.

"Your names were in the newspaper article? Remember? Come on. Let's sort this out." Liam opened the door and went into the living room, ghosts following behind him.

Brit and Seth both jumped up and moved as far back as they could get without jumping over the couch. Neither one could speak.

James and Sarah looked around at the floor. It took Liam a minute to figure it out.

"No, Mildred's out somewhere, chasing mice or something."

The ghosts relaxed slightly, shifting their attention to Seth.

"Wwwhhhhhhaaat are they doing here," Brit could hardly breathe.

"Yeah, I'll second that," Seth said without taking his eyes off the ghosts. He'd seen them for years, but never this close.

"I thought maybe we could clear the air." Liam said matter-of-factly.

The Mistaken Haunting of Seth Harrison

"About what?" Seth asked, still not taking his eyes off James and Sarah.

"About who killed them! What else would I be talking about?"

"Yes, of course," Brit agreed keeping an eye on both Liam and the ghosts. She addressed them directly. "We found evidence that might indicate an alternate scenario."

Liam pulled out the library copies and laid them out on the table.

Brit continued, "It appears that there were two other murders about the same time you died. We're not sure exactly because you weren't found until four weeks later." Brit crinkled up her nose at the idea of rotting bodies in the woods. "Do you know when you died?"

Sarah looked at James, said something no one could hear and then held up eight fingers, then four.

"Eight four, is that it?" Seth asked, coming out of his shock. "August forth?"

Brit gasped. "That's the same day of the other murders." She went over to the articles. "See here." She pointed to the Borden article which had a large photo of the house underneath the headlines *Brutal Murderer Stabs Borden Family to Death. Daughter Lizzie is Prime Suspect.*

Sarah swooned at the site of the photo. James stepped in, but both were unsettled. Their vapory bodies were rippling with little waves. They were silently talking a mile a minute.

Liam, Seth and Brit looked back and forth at each other, then back at the ghosts.

"What are they saying?" Seth asked, staring at the ghosts.

Marie LeClaire

"How am I supposed to know?" Liam barked at him then grabbed a paper off the table. "James, Sarah, does this house mean something to you?" Liam held up a photo of the Borden house.

Rapid nods from both confirmed it.

Liam shook his head. "Damn, how can we communicate?"

"They used a spray can before." Seth turned to James and Sarah. "Can you help one of us write out the answers?"

Shaking heads responded.

"I believe it will take too much energy from them," Liam said.

Nods of confirmation. Then Sarah started an animated charade. She held her arms out to indicate a large round body, then she stroked her chin, pulling her vapor into a long point, and then finally, she puckered up her face pointing to her mouth. Everyone jumped in.

"Beach ball."

"Fat."

"Beard."

"Ugly face."

"Wrinkles."

"Eating something."

"Eating something that doesn't taste good.""

"Eating something sour."

"Sour."

"Sour Puss!" It was Brit who hit it on the nose.

Sarah was jumping up and down with excitement.

"You want to go talk to Sour Puss with us," Liam articulated. "Do you think he'll help us?"

Nods.

"Okay. Seth, are you working tomorrow?"

The Mistaken Haunting of Seth Harrison

"No."

"Brit, have anything at school you can't miss?"

"No."

"Let's meet tomorrow." Liam turned to the ghosts.

They were looking at Liam with dissatisfied frowns, waving hands at themselves and shrugging their shoulders as if asking a question.

"What?" Liam asked.

They kept motioning.

Seth stepped in. "I think they want you to ask them if they're available tomorrow."

Liam sighed. "Okay. Sorry for the assumption. Are you both available tomorrow?"

They both stood a little taller, straightened out their clothes and nodded yes.

"Very well. Do you have any idea if Sour Puss will be around?"

They shrugged.

"We'll have to give it a try then. How about tomorrow at 3 pm?"

Nods.

"And you won't try to kill Seth until then?"

Seth gasped.

The ghosts nodded.

"Very well. We'll meet you there. In the back near your graves if that's alright. It's far enough from the road to be out of sight."

Nods.

Just then, Mildred came strolling in through her personal door from the patio. James grabbed Sarah and went straight to the ceiling.

"Wow. What's going on?" Seth asked.

"It's Mildred. Hello Millie. Nice of you to join us."

Marie LeClaire

"Why are they up there?" Brit pointed curiously to the ceiling.

"Animals like cats and dogs are quite dangerous to ghosts. Their teeth and claws can cause serious damage and even death of sorts to a ghost."

"Ghosts can die?" Seth was incredulous. "Aren't they already dead?"

"Not entirely dead. Mildred can you please leave our guests alone."

"Mmmrrrowww."

"That was a yes." Liam addressed his comments to the ceiling but the trail of vapor was already half-way out through the door jam.

"Tomorrow it is, then."

Liam was fixing dinner while Brit was at the table, Mildred perched on her lap soaking up a good scratching.

"I don't understand the Links," Seth scratched his head. "Why are they here? And why would they connect a cemetery and state hospital?" He was seated at the counter between the kitchen and the dining room.

"Good questions," Liam turned and waved a spatula. "The truth is no one knows a lot about the Links, who created them or why. We do know, or we think we know, that they've been around for hundreds of years. When they were first created, the state hospital and graveyard might not have been there. That leaves the Native Americans or.... someone else."

"What do you mean *someone else*?" Brit piped up.

"Witches, ghosts, aliens, ancient beings we have no knowledge of, unmanifest spirit world kinds of things. When you stop being limited by your senses, the possibilities are endless."

"You're serious," Seth's usual skepticism was showing.

"Quite. The things we don't understand infinitely outnumber the things we do."

Seth kept poking. "And there's this whole global secret society that knows all about this stuff?"

"Well, a couple of secret societies that I'm aware of here in the US. Neither one knows much except that there's power in controlling the Links. Then there are others, like yourselves, that are, shall we say, unaffiliated."

"How did I become an Opener?"

"Unknown."

"Were my parents Openers?"

"Unknown."

"What's this pendant thing I have."

"Unknown. At least to me. I've never seen one before."

"Damn, Liam, what do you know?"

Liam turned from the stove and gave Seth a look of adult disapproval.

Seth sighed. "Sorry. I'm just feeling like I'm back to being crazy and you're all just crazy with me."

Brit came to the rescue. "Yeah, and I think we're all a little hungry, too. Let's eat."

Chapter 27

Puss was watching from behind a mausoleum as the Opener showed back up at the graveyard with his two friends. What were they doing back here? Closing the Link? Suddenly two ghosts popped up right behind him, sending him vaporing into the air in response. He looked down to see James and Sarah.

With steam coming out of his ears, he charged back down. "What's wrong with you! You got no manners?"

"Sorry Puss. I guess we weren't thinking," James said.

"I guess not." Puss shook his head.

"Are you a little jumpy today, Puss?" Sarah asked.

"Maybe I am."

"We just came through from Bridgewater," Sarah explained. "Isn't it exciting to have a new Link?"

Puss ignored the small talk. "What are you doing here?"

"We want you to talk to that guy for us." James pointed in Seth's direction.

"Why?"

"He's that one we've been telling you about."

Puss didn't seem surprised.

"You know him, Puss?" James asked.

"He came through here the other day. He's the one who opened the Link."

"Whhhaaattt? You're joking with us." Sarah gasped.

Marie LeClaire

"No joke. Did it without a bit of trouble either."

"What's that mean, Puss? Who is he?"

"I don't know, James. But if he's your man, it's going to be harder to kill him than you think."

"We're not sure he is, Puss. That's why we're here. They have some kind of newspaper story about some other murders the same day as ours."

"They do, do they?"

"What do you say, Puss. Will you talk for us?"

"Let's do it, then. I haven't got all day." Puss put on his usual show of insincere irritation, then floated over to the three visitors, followed closely by James and Sarah.

Liam stepped forward as the three ghosts approached.

"Good afternoon, Mr. Puss," Liam greeted him. "And James and Sarah. Thank you for coming."

"These kids tell me you've got things to talk about." Puss tipped his head backward indicating James and Sarah.

Liam followed suit, nodding back at Seth and Brit. "These kids tell me the same thing."

"They say you have information about their murderer."

"We believe we have a plausible alternative story. When we showed the article to James and Sarah, they seemed to know something more, but for obvious reasons, that's as far as we got."

"Let's see what you have."

Liam reached back to Brit who handed him the Borden article with the photo. "James and Sarah told us that they died on August 4th, 1892, however their bodies were not discovered for some time afterwards. It was assumed that Simeon Harrison, a possible ancestor of Seth here, murdered them."

"That's how I recall it." Puss confirmed.

"James and Sarah died on the same day that the Bordens were killed and in the same manner."

"You don't say. Why didn't they figure that out back then?"

"The bodies were too decomposed to ascertain a conclusive time of death and they were just two drifters as far as anyone knew. It was easy to assume their friend killed them and close the case. No offense." Liam waved an apology to James and Sarah. "But when I showed them this picture of the other murders, they got very excited."

Puss looked at the photo of the Borden house then motioned the two ghosts to step forward. "Does this house mean something to you?"

Sarah and James both started talking at once. "Hey!" Puss yelled. They both stopped at once.

"James." Puss pointed.

"We were with Simeon that day, scamming our way down to Virginia. We stopped in Fall River and got lodging in the barn of that house. Borden, I think was the name."

"Yes, it was Borden," Sarah jumped in. Puss shot her a look and she instantly quieted down.

James went on. "The accommodations weren't free though. Sarah got work inside the house and Simeon and I worked the barn. We were going to stay the night, but late in the morning. Sarah came running out saying we have to go, now, so we quick packed up our stuff and what we could steal and ran off here to camp for the night. Then we were dead."

Puss was considering this story while Sarah was bouncing up and down, wringing her hands into vapor, trying to keep quiet. Finally, Puss waved at her indicating she could speak.

Marie LeClaire

"I got a lot of cash and a few pieces of jewelry from the house and figured we were better off leaving earlier than later in case we were found out. Now that I'm thinking about it, there was something strange going on upstairs. I heard an unusual thudding noise, and my skin started to creep. That's when I grabbed my goods and ran out."

"Yeah," James agreed. "Simeon was acting off all day too, fretting about something. Said he had the worries and he kept grabbing at that necklace he used to wear. I bet it's the same one Seth wears."

Puss held up his hand indicating that they should stop. He turned to the others.

"They say that they were with Simeon Harrison when they robbed that house. They took off by late morning and camped out back of here. Next thing they knew, they were dead and Simeon was gone. They say he wore something around his neck, same as Seth here. They think it's the same one."

All eyes turned to Seth. Self-consciously he reached for the crystal under his shirt. "My mom gave it to me the day she died. That's all I know about it except for the last few weeks when it's been acting funny."

Liam kept them on track and away from conversation about the pendant. "The Bordens were murdered in the same manner and on the same day as James and Sarah. Doesn't that sound a little too coincidental?"

"I can see that." Puss concurred. "So, who would want to kill both the Bordens and these two?"

"That is the question. Certainly not Simeon as far as I can see." Liam added.

Puss turned to Sarah. "What did you take from the house?"

"Cash from a tin under the mattress, three pretty hair pins," Sarah smiled at the memory and fussed with her hair, "and a brass broach with scrolls and jewels in the center."

"How big was the broach?" Puss asked.

"About this big." Sarah held up her thumb and forefinger almost touching, making a circle about the size of a half dollar.

Puss turned back to Liam. "Sarah said she took cash, hair pins and a broach with jewels on it about that big." He pointed to Sarah who raised her hand again to indicate the size.

Seth leapt forward. "Like this?" He held out the broach they took from the barn the day before.

Liam snapped at him. "Put that away. I thought I told you to leave it at the house!"

Seth stuffed it back in his jacket pocket defiantly. "So. Something made me take it anyway. I had a feeling."

"Lovely," Liam rolled his eyes. When he turned back around, he saw Puss who had floated a little higher and was staring him down. Sarah was jumping up and down and pointing at the broach.

"What do you have there, Liam? Looks like the same item that Sarah stole a hundred years ago. And it's a Caller Coin. You think I didn't notice? It's turning the tables back to Simeon, don't you think?"

Chapter 28

Liam sneered at Seth before turning back to Puss. "When we were here yesterday, we toured the Borden house. This Caller Coin was unceremoniously nailed to the wall as an artifact found in the barn during a recent renovation." Liam explained.

"And?" Puss insisted.

"And we liberated it."

"I see." Puss floated back down but continued to eye the group suspiciously.

Liam continued to explain. "I'm not surprised the Bordens were Coin holders. I understand they were a nasty lot."

"Not all of them, but Andrew was certainly a hateful goat," agreed Puss. "Mean just for the sake of being mean. They had a Guardian out here at the gate round the clock. It was unnerving for everyone. So how did something that Sarah stole get back to the barn of the house she stole it from?"

"And how did Simeon escape," Liam added.

"It's still possible that Simeon double-crossed them, stole the cash and goods and took off while they were sleeping," Puss posited. "Or maybe even took up with Charles and his beast after the murders."

James started nodding his head angrily.

Seth responded, "He did not. He wasn't that kind of guy."

James continued to argue without audio, both young men posturing at each other.

Brit jumped to Simeon's defense. "The article said there was an empty jug of booze found at the campsite."

James got suddenly quiet at this revelation. Puss turned to the two ghosts.

James confessed under Puss's glare. "Yeah, Puss, I sort of recall there being some drinking going on."

"Uh-huh," Puss nodded. "And how much exactly?"

"It might have been the whole jug," Sarah admitted.

"Uh-huh. So, you weren't so much sleeping as you were passed out?"

"Well, that could be true." James nodded.

"And how much did Simeon have to drink?"

They both thought for a minute. Sarah shook her head. "I don't think he had hardly any. He was restless, irritated. That necklace of his was itching him bad. He didn't feel good about it."

"Yeah," James added. "He went off for a walk to clear his head."

Puss turned to Liam. "They admit that the two of them were good and drunk that night, with Simeon abstaining. It doesn't sway things one way or the other. Could be said that Simeon didn't drink because he had other plans."

"Or, if there are Guardians involved, it's not hard to believe that they committed both sets of murders," Liam added. "Maybe Simeon got away because he wasn't drunk."

There was a scurry of activity in the cemetery as birds and squirrels scattered in all directions.

"What's happening?" Liam asked. "Brit?"

The Mistaken Haunting of Seth Harrison

"According to the squirrels there's a terrible storm approaching."

"That's ridiculous. There isn't a cloud in the sky." Liam argued.

"That's all I'm getting. Storm. Run. Wind. Nuts. Run."

Suddenly a strong wind picked up, growing in intensity until it threatened to blow everyone over. Liam, Seth and Brit took cover behind a large tree, hanging on to it and each other. The ghosts, particularly susceptible to the elements, were already taking cover in whatever container they could find that wouldn't blow over. Puss headed straight for a large cement planter that marked the grave of a founding father, the other two found cover in a cement trash container nearby.

The wind increased, whipping up debris from the cemetery grounds, forming a funnel that touched down nearby and held itself in place. In the center appeared a smoky vapor-like apparition. The wind died down and the leaves fell, revealing a ghost standing about fifteen feet away.

Everyone stopped and stared for a long moment, then James let out a yell. "Simeon, you no-good-for-nothing, traitorous, thieving con man." James was heading straight over to the new arrival when Puss vaporized between the two.

"James! What are you doing?" Puss demanded. James turned to vapor and made a hard U-turn to avoid the collision, then came back again to stand in front of Puss.

"What are you doing, Puss! That's the no-good son of a bitch that killed us and I'm about to get even!" James waved his arms angrily. Puss stood steady, staring James down with a stern look. James backed up a few paces.

183

Puss turned to the new arrival. "What's your name, son."

Simeon said nothing. He just stood there, stunned, confused and a little wobbly.

Puss shook his head slowly. "Oh-oh. I've seen that look many times. Simeon here is a new ghost."

"What do you mean a new ghost?" James demanded.

"Just what I said, a new ghost. You remember what it was like."

"Well, not really. Dang, that was 100 years ago!" James' foot turned to clouds of smoke as he stomped it into the ground.

"Excuse me," Liam interrupted. "Are you saying this ghost is Simeon Harrison?"

"According to this nit-wit." Puss pointed a thumb toward James.

Everyone turned to Seth as if waiting for confirmation.

"How am I supposed to know?" Seth threw his hands up.

"Mr. Puss, if I may." It was Liam again. "What do you mean a new ghost? Simeon has been dead for many years even under the best scenario."

"Not newly dead, newly ghosted. I can't say I know how it works but I've seen this before. Simeon has just awoken from the dead."

Liam rolled his eyes to the heavens and mumbled under his breath, "Could this get any more complicated?"

They all got quiet again as they turned to Simeon. Puss floated slowly over to him.

"Is your name Simeon?"

The ghost just nodded.

"Do you know where you are?"

Simeon shook his head slowly, keeping his eyes on James and Sarah.

"Do you know these two people?"

A nod in reply.

"Do you remember what happened to them?"

Another nod, then finally Simeon spoke. "Is this hell?"

"No, son. It is not. Why would you ask?"

"Because the thing that killed them was dispatched from the devil himself."

Unable to wait any longer, Seth stepped forward. "Is that my – uh – uncle?"

Simeon turned to Seth, each staring back at the other. Both automatically reached for the pendant they wore. When Simeon didn't find it, he pointed to Seth. Seth pulled the crystal out of his shirt and showed it to Simeon.

Simeon was confused. "That's mine."

Puss continued very gently. "Maybe that was yours many years ago but now it belongs to that boy, Seth Harrison."

Simeon staggered backward. "I don't understand. Where am I?"

"Brace yourself, son. You're in Fall River in the year 2018. And you're dead."

Simeon's wispy legs buckled and turned to cloudy mist. Down he went. Puss rushed over to him. He snaked one arm under one of Simeon's arms, around his back and under the other arm, then helped him to the nearest headstone. Simeon fell to the ground, leaning up against the stone. "Come over here, Seth. Sit with Simeon. He needs a little bit of energy, and you won't hardly miss it." Puss waved him over.

Seth was terrified. He looked to Liam for guidance.

Marie LeClaire

"Go on." Liam nodded assurance that he didn't wholly feel.

Seth walked over to Puss and Simeon. "What should I do?"

"Nothing. Just sit beside him for a few minutes. Really, it won't hurt a bit. Your life force will help energize him."

Seth squatted down beside the ghost, putting one knee on the ground. Simeon looked up at him, giving what appeared to be a sigh and a nod.

Puss turned to the others, both human and ghost. "I've seen new ghosts before. It takes them a while to get their bearings. They have no idea what just happened to them or why they're here. And before you ask me, neither do I. I just know it's a rough transition and he needs some rest. Simeon getting energy from Seth proves they're family somehow."

James was the first to speak. "When can I kill him, Puss?" He was jumping around on his toes. Sarah was restraining him.

Puss translated for the humans. "James wants to know when he can kill him?"

"No!" Seth yelled and started a charge towards James that was thwarted by Liam who darted over to his side and grabbed his upper arm tightly.

"Ouch! Let me go!" Seth struggled for his freedom but the more he struggled, the tighter the grip. Liam's strength surprised him. In the end, Seth didn't so much free himself as Liam let go, once he calmed down. Seth returned to his position beside Simeon but continued to stare down James.

"Now, now. Let's all stay calm," Puss waved his hands. More departed had quietly appeared, taking up

The Mistaken Haunting of Seth Harrison

defensive positions behind Puss. The show of power was not lost on Liam.

"Yes. I agree." Liam nodded to Puss. He leaned down and took Seth by the arm again, more gently this time. He didn't want any sudden move to spark a conflict. "No need for things to escalate. If Simeon needs time to recover, perhaps it's best if we continue our conversation another time."

"Yes. I think under the circumstances, that would be wise." Puss remained perfectly still as did the other ghosts.

"Seth, Brit, let's go." Liam backed away, not taking his eyes off Puss and the others.

Seth rose slowly and walked with Liam back to Brit, who had kept her distance. Almost immediately Simeon moaned and a slight vapor trailed in Seth's direction, landing directly on the pendant.

"Wait," Puss held up a hand to Seth who stopped instantly. "Simeon, what's going on?"

"I don't know, just that when he walked away, I felt really …," Simeon struggled to find words to describe what was happening, "misty."

Puss turned to Seth. "It would appear that the pendant is Simeon's touchstone."

Liam looked up to the heavens again. "Apparently it can."

"Seth," Puss directed. "Come back and stay with Simeon for the time being and let's figure this out."

Chapter 29

Cameron Borden was driving a Sheriff's patrol car and was in full uniform from the prison when he pulled into the cemetery parking lot. He was just in time to see the wind funnel that deposited Simeon into the present day. He watched the exchange between ghosts and humans from a distance. When the dust settled, he walked through the cemetery, shoulders back, chest puffed up, and wearing a barely concealed side arm.

Puss moved to position himself between Borden and the departed as Cameron approached them.

Liam was surprised to recognize Sgt. Borden. "That's the guard from the prison. Cameron Borden."

"I'm familiar," was all Puss said as they waited.

"Puss," Cameron said as he approached.

"Borden," Puss replied.

"What's happening here?" Cameron sneered, making eye contact with everyone, adding an extra huff of disgust at Liam.

"Oh, let me see," Puss replied. "That would be none of your damn business."

"Really? Because I thought the Departed and the Legion had an *understanding*."

"We understand that you do whatever the hell you want."

Marie LeClaire

"Yeah. That would be it." He sneered at Puss. He addressed Liam without turning to face him. "What are *you* doing here, McMurty?"

Liam stepped toward him, refusing to be intimidated. "Visiting a relative. You?"

Cameron turned to him. "I heard there was an Opener in town."

"We heard the same thing," Liam replied.

Cameron took a step toward Seth.

Puss and Liam both positioned themselves in between.

"Really?" Cameron remarked, moving his hand to his firearm. "Are we doing this?" He stared at them both. They stared back.

"What do you want, Cameron?" Puss demanded.

"I want to know how you opened the Link," he growled.

"Well, if you were as close to the Legion as you say you are," Puss stroked his beard, "you'd know that it wasn't me who opened it."

"No one's been able to open that Link for a hundred years."

"A hundred and twenty-five," Puss corrected.

Cameron surveyed the group again, noticing Seth's attachment to the new ghost. "I heard it was a boy." Cameron was fishing, but Seth and the girl were the only unknowns.

No one replied.

Cameron took a step toward Seth and Simeon. "How is it that a *boy* could unlock a Link that the Masters of the Legion couldn't get open?"

"I guess it's because the Legion doesn't have any more Openers." Puss was calmly angry. "I guess it's because you idiots killed all the Consortium's Openers and then your own up and died. Geniuses, you are."

Cameron turned on Puss quickly. "Be careful, Puss. I could kill you where you stand."

Puss immediately vaporized, shot upward, turning in the air and shot back down, reforming directly behind Cameron.

"And what if I'm standing here?" he taunted him.

Cameron spun back around, reached into his pocket and pulled out a Caller Coin. A shadowy beast in a black hooded cloak appeared at his side. Cameron took a step toward Puss.

Just then, streams of smoky vapor arose from behind headstones in all directions, heads and torsos propped on tails of vapor. Fifty or so by Liam's count, ready to move in. Cameron scanned the cemetery, side to side. A flare of anger crossed his face before he dismissed the Guardian with the jerk of his hand. The creature was gone as quickly as it had appeared.

"You have no idea the power of the Legion. This isn't over," Cameron sneered. Then he turned on his heel and headed back to his car.

The crowd held their ground as they watched Cameron walk away.

Puss addressed the departed, "Thanks everyone. It looks like things are going to get interesting, but we're probably good for now."

One by one the dearly departed drifted back from where they came. All except James, Sarah, and Simeon.

Liam exhaled audibly. "Thank you, Puss."

"My pleasure. I love putting that sniveling rat in his place."

"You know him then?"

"He comes by here every so often, boasting, prideful, thinking he's scaring us. I usually let him think so, so I can surprise him when I need to, like today."

James rushed up to them. "That's him, Puss That's the one. The one I have the burning desire to kill. That's him." James was pointing after Cameron.

"Borden? That man's kin was the cousin of Andrew Borden," Puss told him. "I'm beginning to think Liam's story might ring true. If a Borden beast killed you, it would make sense, you having the burning."

"Ouch."

Everyone turned to look as Seth grabbed at his pendant.

Simeon was still leaning up against the stone, eyes wide and nodding slowly.

"Is that what you saw here that night?" Puss asked him.

Simeon continued to nod.

He looked over at Liam. "James seems to think maybe the Bordens had something to do with their killing."

Liam thought about this for a minute. "Let's say someone with a Borden Coin, turned the Guardian onto Andrew and Abby, realized Andrew's Coin was missing and went looking for it."

Puss shrugged. "Could be true, but only *could be*."

Sarah floated up right behind Puss. "You really think it was a Borden and his Guardian that killed us?"

"It's possible," Puss was nodding and stroking his beard. "In which case, Cameron is your man."

Chapter 30

Puss insisted they take Simeon with them when Seth refused to relinquish possession of the crystal. The new ghost laid beside Seth in the back seat of Liam's car, barely awake, for the ride home.

Now inside the house, he was completely alert – staring, pointing and trying to touch everything in the house. Still unable to communicate verbally, Simeon would point at something and either Seth or Brit would tell him what it was and explained how it worked.

When he pointed to the big screen TV, Liam interrupted, "You might hold off on that for now. It might be a little too much for him."

"Sure. Good idea," Seth agreed. "Besides, I have a ton of questions of my own."

"I can't imagine how you'll get them answered," Brit said. "We can't hear a word he's saying."

"I thought about that, but if he can read, maybe we can work something out."

Simeon was listening and excitedly nodded his head.

"Looks like that's a yes. What are you thinking?" Liam asked.

"Well, we could put together a letter board. Simeon doesn't have to write or speak. He can point to letters and spell things out." Seth was rummaging around the dining

Marie LeClaire

area. "It sounds a little tedious, but if we keep it simple, we might get through a few questions."

"What are you looking for? Don't touch that!" Liam yelled, as Seth started opening cabinet doors.

"Liam, do you have a chalk board around here? I thought I saw one."

"No. Leave that alone!" Liam was grabbing things out of Seth's hands. "You'll mess things up."

Seth and Brit stopped what they were doing. They looked at Liam, suppressing a smile.

"Really?" Brit asked.

"There's an order to things around here?" Seth asked.

"Yes." Liam put things back to where Seth had taken them from. "Sort of. What are you looking for?"

"A board big enough to write out the alphabet in a way that Simeon can point to letters."

"Here." Liam walked into the kitchen and produced the top of the pizza box.

"Okay. That'll do. Magic markers? Not really magic ones though. You know. Just regular magic markers."

Liam was looking at him, trying to figure out if he was serious, when Seth busted out in a grin.

"Cute. In the drawer of the hutch with the non-magical pens and scotch tape." Liam reluctantly gave up a grin of his own.

Seth returned to the dining room table with cardboard, markers, paper and a pen.

"You write down the letters as we go," he said, sliding the pen and paper to Brit.

She slid it right back at him. "Do I look like your secretary?" She crossed her arms over her chest and stared at him.

The Mistaken Haunting of Seth Harrison

"No. Not at all. Sorry. No," Seth was tripping over himself to apologize.

"Okay, then." She reached out for the pen and paper. "In that case, I'd love to help."

Seth stood perfectly still for a moment while his brain tried to figure out what just happened.

"Just go with it, Seth," Liam coached him from the kitchen.

"Okay. Thanks, Brit."

Seth grabbed a marker and the pizza lid and wrote out the alphabet, saying each letter out loud until he realized he was doing it, and stopped.

Brit was nodding along with him. "Add the numbers, just in case."

When the board was done, he propped it up within easy reach of Simeon and in plain sight of he and Brit.

"Good thinking Seth. Let's see how well we do." Liam had come around the table to watch.

Seth started asking questions. "So, you're my great-great-great-or-something-like-that uncle?"

Simeon shrugged.

"Right. He wouldn't know that," Brit added.

"Right," Seth agreed.

"You saw who killed James and Sarah?"

A nod.

"Why didn't they kill you?"

Simeon pointed to the letter *I* then slashed his hand.

"I chopped. I slashed. I cut," Seth offered.

Simeon shook his head and waved a hand as if to erase it.

"I think he means that I is the end of the word," Liam offered.

Simeon nodded.

195

Marie LeClaire

"Okay. I what?" Seth called out the letters as Brit wrote them down.

"H-I-D. I hid. You hid?"

A nod.

"R-A-N F-A-S-T."

"I don't blame you. We saw the pictures."

"What is the pendent?" It was Liam who asked.

A shrug.

"G-R-A-N-D-F-A-T-H-E-R G-A-V-E M-E. D-I-E-D B-E-F-O-R-E H-E T-O-L-D M-E W-H-A-T IT W-A-S." Seth called out letters as Brit wrote it down then read it back.

"Grandfather gave me. Died before he told me what it was," Brit announced.

"Where were your parents," Seth asked.

Simeon made a slicing motion across his throat.

"Dead? Well, obviously dead now. But dead then?" Seth asked.

A nod.

"Murdered?" Liam asked.

Simeon nodded slowly.

And so it went. Simeon spelled, Seth called out the letters, Brit read it back, as Simeon told the story of coming to Fall River and his escape to New Hampshire.

"Where did you go in New Hampshire?" again it was Liam.

"Found sisters. Concord."

Liam was firing the questions now. "Did you live there? Marry? Have children?"

Simeon faded for a moment.

"Stop it, Liam. You're exhausting him," Brit complained.

"This is important," he said crossly. "Simeon?"

The Mistaken Haunting of Seth Harrison

Simeon closed his eyes and scrunched up his face trying to remember.

When he opened his eyes, a look of surprise crossed his face as he nodded.

"Two boys. Died age 35," Brit read.

Simeon pointed to himself and pulled a hand across his throat as his form started to melt into vapor.

"Liam, why are you doing this? It's hurting him," Seth complained.

"Yeah," Brit agreed.

"It has to do with something I read. Where was it? Millie would know. Where is she anyway?"

Just then, Mildred strolled in through her door. Her back was immediately up when she saw Simeon. Hissing, she got up on her hind legs and took a swing at him, claws bared.

"NOOOOOOO!" everyone cried, but not before Millie frayed the edge of Simeon's leg, causing him to jerk his feet up off the floor and out of immediate reach.

Mildred slowly backed down. "*Meeeeoooooorrrw.*"

"Yes. Thank you, Millie," Liam said calmly. "This is our guest, Simeon Harrison. Sorry we couldn't warn you."

"*Mmmmrrreeeeoow rrrrww.*"

"Yes. We think he's Seth's great-many-times uncle," Brit informed her.

"Millie, where is that old Consortium manuscript we were reading the other day?"

"*Mrrrrrw mmeow mow.*"

"Right." Liam retrieved a cardboard cylinder from behind a stack of boxes and tipped rolled up papers onto the table.

"Here it is." He unrolled the hand-written documents. "It was years ago. They were interviewing an elderly

Marie LeClaire

Consortium member to make sure that they recorded all the information he had before he died. He started mumbling about some old Links lore. They weren't even sure he was coherent. Something about the seventh son becoming the next Opener."

He ran his finger down the page. "Right here," Liam read. "... for each seventh son shall be the new Opener." He looked up, recognition dawning on his face. "He wasn't talking about a seventh sibling. He was talking about seven *generations*! The seventh generation produces a Link Opener. Seth, I don't think Simeon is your uncle. I think he's your great-times-six grandfather. His father was an Opener. Probably killed in the Eradication by the King's Legion."

"What!" Seth grabbed his head as if to stop it from exploding.

"It's the only thing that makes sense. Simeon's parents were killed by the Legion while he was away. They likely thought there were no male heirs. They let your sisters live because they were of no consequence either way. It must be transferred through the men."

"*Mrreeeoooww, mrrww, meoe.*"

"Yes. And if we figured it out, they did too." Liam's voice had a sense of urgency.

"Who is they? And what have they figured out?" demanded Brit.

Just then, the phone rang. Liam looked at the number then headed out to the patio with his phone. "Yes. Fay. What can I do for you?...Yes….No…I don't think a lockdown is really….Oh?... Still might be an overreaction….I'm more than capable of keeping the boy safe…If all this is true, then we are going to need a little more than academic bluster… This is just another example

The Mistaken Haunting of Seth Harrison

of the Consortium's unwillingness to act. Are you going to let us all die as well? All except Seth I suppose...Fine. Two days." Liam paced back and forth before heading back inside.

"Fay, the Consortium's Chairperson, has suggested we initiate lockdown protocols. Millie, can you see to it?"

Mildred let out a mew and jumped onto the table, then to the buffet, then to the top of the bookcase. Walking down to the end, she reached up and tapped an almost invisible button on the wall. Thin gray metal rods dropped down across all doors and windows.

Liam rolled up the scrolls, collected a few other manuscripts and secured them in the cabinet with a lock that had a slight glow to it.

"Liam, what is happening?" Seth asked, not sure if he should be panicking or not.

"Just precaution. Give me the Caller Coin."

"Not until you tell me what's going on."

Liam hedged. "The Consortium believes that you might be in danger. Now give me the Coin so I can secure it."

"No."

Seth's open defiance caused Liam to pause.

"Why should I give you the only thing that has any power to protect us? Or am I wrong?"

"Look, kid. You don't know how to use that thing." It was the first time Liam had used a pejorative tone.

"And you do?" he challenged him back.

"Not first hand, no."

"Then I'll just keep it."

"This is no time to argue!" Liam insisted.

"Then stop arguing."

Marie LeClaire

Liam realized he had made the fatal mistake of arguing with a teenager.

"Fine. Keep it."

Seth stuck his hand in his pocket, feeling for the Coin, and immediately felt unsure about what he'd just argued for.

"Liam, what are these rods?" Brit asked.

"They have a specific magnetic frequency that prevents Guardians from opening portals into the house."

"So, we're just supposed to sit here and wait?" she asked.

"Yes. For the time being. Until I can think of something else."

Chapter 31

"Wait. Was the pottery shard mine or yours?" Brit asked. They were halfway through the first morning of lockdown.

"Mine. The old house key is yours." Seth replied. Simeon indicated a square on the checker board and Seth shifted his piece for him.

"I'm about done with creative checkers." Brit leaned back and sighed. Only two hours into lockdown and she was getting fidgety. "Liam, I'm losing my mind. Let's do something."

Liam lifted his head up from an old book he was studying. "I'm working on it." He had been scouring through old lore looking for anything about Openers as he could find, which wasn't much. He was beginning to understand that the next Opener, presumably Seth, was going to be a huge player in the years to come. As of this moment, none of the original family lines would produce an Opener ever again, thanks to the Legion. Seth had just become the most important asset in the Linkage world. Liam was hoping to use that to his advantage.

The departed were now a wildcard though. Based on the show of force in the cemetery yesterday, there was a growing power there. Individually, a ghost had very little self-advocacy, but organized? Liam was imagining how they could do some damage, jamming machinery, stopping hearts, pushing large objects onto people. Liam had read accounts of ghosts being shredded in the past, but not killed. He reasoned that what they lacked in skills or resources, they made up for in numbers. He needed to know their allegiance.

"We need to go back to the cemetery," he announced.

Brit perked up. "What for?"

"We need to know where the departed stand."

Simeon drifted around the furniture to look straight at Liam.

"Or float, I guess," Liam corrected himself.

"What do you mean *where they stand?*" asked Seth.

"Old hostilities are brewing. We need to be ready."

"What about the lockdown?"

"A manipulation by the Consortium to buy them some time. Well, it bought us a little time as well. Now, we need a plan."

"Wait a minute!" Seth sat up in his recliner and leaned forward. "There is no *us.* And there is no *we.* I'm not any part of this."

"Me either," stated Brit.

Simeon stood taller with his hands on his hips in agreement.

"Don't you get it!" Liam growled back. "You *are all* a part of it. You are *the* part of it. You don't get a choice."

"Hell, I don't," Seth insisted.

"You are the first Opener to appear in a hundred years. You think people are going to let you walk away?"

Seth and Brit looked at each other, assimilating the information. They looked at Simeon who turned his palms up and shrugged his shoulders.

"But I don't want it."

"Look at it this way. You have something that two very powerful organizations want, control of the entire

The Mistaken Haunting of Seth Harrison

Linkage, around the world, and beyond maybe. Who knows? You are not walking away."

"What about the Consortium?" Brit asked.

"They are friendly enough but ineffective, repeatedly refusing to arm against the Legion. If push comes to shove, and it will, the Legion is willing to kill for what it wants."

"Shit." Seth shook his head.

"What are you thinking?" Brit asked Liam.

"There still might be a wildcard here with the departed. I suggest we head to the cemetery and have a talk with Sour Puss."

***

Cameron was on a video call with three of his cousins and a couple of buddies from the prison, all had Legion affiliations.

He had their attention. "The Fall River Link is open."

"Yeah. So what?" his cousin, Derek countered.

"We have to do something about it. That's what."

"Have you heard something from the Commander?" asked another.

"We can't always wait for Command to take action. They're willing to wait around to *see what happens.* They've all gone soft."

"Yeah," said cousin Basil. "There's an Opener around and we need to have him. We can't be waiting around for people to pick sides."

"What exactly are you getting at, Cameron?" asked a guard.

"I'm talking about taking action. We need to straight-up show that kid whose side he needs to be on."

"Defying Command?" someone asked.

Marie LeClaire

"Taking command," Basil clarified.

"I heard he's just a kid. With a kid girlfriend," Derek argued. "What are you talking about? Killing him?"

"No, stupid. He's a freakin' Opener. I just want to emphasize the benefits of joining with us. Ha ha." This got a chuckle from the group, encouraging him to continue. "Maybe point out that his girlfriend might be better off that way."

"Hey. Maybe I could *initiate* her," added another.

Derek tried to be the voice of reason. "Maybe we should let Command handle this. They probably know things we don't."

"What's wrong, Derek? You satisfied waiting around, doing nothing, waiting for a bunch of old men to die before any of us can take some responsibility in this business? Well, I'm not." Cameron was pounding his chest while he talked.

The others followed suit in agreement.

Basil challenged Derek. "So, are you in or out?"

Derek felt the pressure to go along. Despite all the holes he saw in their logic, he couldn't see a way out.

"Alright. What's the plan?"

Cameron got serious. "I got a feeling those ghosts are going to be trouble so the first thing we do is go put them back in their place. Dead. Ha ha. Or as dead as they can be. There's six of us with three Guardians at our disposal. Armed with pitch forks and rakes we should be able to shred the lot of them and still be home for dinner."

There were grunts of agreement from them all. Shredding meant that the departed would be out of commission for at least several weeks while they separated out their vapor from each other and regained strength.

"When?" someone asked.

The Mistaken Haunting of Seth Harrison

"Today. At the cemetery at 1600."
They all agreed.

***

Marilisa checked off the last box on her spread sheet. "All accounted for, Fay. The last counselor just booked plane fare to Providence. Everyone should be at the airport by 2 pm. I reserved a van at the terminal rental car hub and Willard will be driving the supplies down from New York in one of our SUVs, meeting you there."

"Excellent work, Marilisa. Thank you."

The phone rang. Marilisa picked it up. "It's Farley, for you."

"Thank you. That will be all for now," Fay replied and waited for Marilisa to close the door behind her.

"Farley. What do you have for me?...I know he's an Opener. Tell me something I don't know, like where he came from...How far back do our records go?...What about the work McMurty was doing?...No! His father. Keep up! I already know what Liam is doing...Very well....No. Head over to London. See what you can find there."

Chapter 32

Liam and his crew arrived at the cemetery in mid-afternoon. As soon as they parked the car, Puss' vapor could be seen at the back of the cemetery. They walked cautiously from the gate, Simeon floating along beside them.

Seth was growing more uncomfortable. "My necklace is vibing like crazy."

"I'm not surprised," Liam replied. "There's a lot of energy here today. Stay alert," Liam cautioned.

Puss waited patiently for them, making no effort to meet them halfway. When they finally arrived, tension could be felt in the air.

"Liam," Puss greeted him.

"Sour Puss," Liam replied.

"What brings you here?"

"It appears that what has been a hundred-year holding pattern is now changing rapidly."

"It would seem so."

"The Consortium and the Legion are both mobilizing."

Puss said nothing.

"Seth, here, seems to be the unfortunate target, through no fault of his own and with no particular allegiance."

"What's your point, Liam?" said Puss.

"It became evident yesterday that the Dearly Departed have not been sitting by idly for the past hundred years. We are interested in discussing where your allegiance lies."

"I could ask you the same."

"My intention, our intention, is simply to protect Seth from either force. He has no interest in getting involved in this business."

"Ha!" Puss bellowed. "Too late for that, I'd say." He looked over at Seth.

Seth stepped boldly forward. "I don't want anything to do with any of this. I just want to live my life, now that I finally have one." He looked over at Brit, who smiled back at him. Then to Simeon, who nodded agreement.

Simeon began to speak silently, except to Puss.

"Simeon tells me he plans to stay with you for the time being. He's hoping that Sarah and James will join you."

"We all just want to be left alone," said Seth.

Puss spoke. "The departed are also not interested in getting between the Legion and the Consortium. If Simeon is willing to go along with the humans, we have no argument."

Liam asked, "Do you have a way to deter interference by the Legion? They're most likely to take an aggressive stance?"

"We can hold our own. And we might get the chance." Puss nodded toward the parking lot where three black SUVs were now parked.

"Great." Liam rolled his eyes skyward.

Cameron and his posse arrived at the cemetery in full stealth gear, dressed in black military uniforms. The common rakes they were carrying seemed comical. They arrived in time to witness the meeting between Puss and Liam from the parking lot.

"Well, this changes things a bit," Cameron said to his team. "Maybe we get two birds with one rake. Ha ha."

"Let's do it," Basil said, coming around the vehicle. "You two with me around this way." He indicated to the left.

"Go," Cameron nodded to Basil. "Derek, you take two around to the right. I'll set up in the rear with these two. Whistle when you're in position," Cameron ordered. "Puss is the kingpin. He's our target. Don't worry about McMurty. He won't challenge the Guardians. He doesn't have it in him."

They split up and quietly surrounded the back side of the cemetery.

Back at the Spencer Abby, Malik was gritting his teeth and growling at a lieutenant who was delivering bad news.

"What the hell is going on! What does that idiot, Cameron, think he's doing? And where is Mildred!"

"A-a-a-h. I don't know, sir. To all of those questions, sir."

"Those Bordens have always been more trouble than they're worth. Get me my gear. I'm going to have to try and salvage this."

"Yes, sir."

There were three short whistles, then six soldiers quietly stepped into view. Weapons at the ready.

"Um. Are they carrying rakes?" Brit asked.

Marie LeClaire

"The tines shred ghosts quickly into damaged unformed vapor," Liam explained, as he looked around at the circle of men.

Puss called out, "You don't want to do this, Cameron."

"Oh, but I do, old man," came the retort. "We want the Opener. And his pretty little friend."

"Not happening," Liam replied.

"Not ever," Seth chimed in with a bravado he didn't feel.

Cameron's group closed in slowly.

"Where's all your misty friends, Puss? Not interested in losing to Legion forces?"

"Not planning to."

Liam spoke softly to Puss, keeping his eyes on the commandos. "I don't know what your plan is, Puss, but now is a good time to run it."

Puss, very slowly, raised his hands, palms up. As he did so, departed started appearing from behind stones and trees. Facing outward, they formed a circle around Puss and the others.

"So, it is." Cameron raised his rake and he and the others picked up the pace. The soldiers positioned their rakes across their bodies as they approached the outer ring of departed. Suddenly and simultaneously, the ghosts shot upward thirty feet, u-turned and, in groups of three, descended directly onto the soldiers, head first, encasing the human as they headed toward the ground. As the ghosts neared the ground, they turned sharply and streamed off at grass level beyond striking distance. In doing so, each ghost was able to pull a small amount of energy out of the humans.

The Mistaken Haunting of Seth Harrison

"Get back," Liam called to Seth and Brit, who complied without a word.

"Liam straightened his long coat and took a solid stance, feet wide apart, bracing for a fight. He looked around only to realize that no one seemed interested in him. Slightly disappointed, he paused to watch the battle.

The soldiers, expecting a frontal or at least horizontal attack, began to swing wildly in front and to the sides, having no effect at all on the ghostly assault. As the first attackers floated away, a second wave of ghosts appeared within seconds and executed the same maneuver, draining a little more energy from Cameron and his crew.

The soldiers were feeling it.

"Call them!" Cameron cried out.

Suddenly, three large creatures dressed in black and carrying pitch forks appeared on the scene. "Try your games on that, you soul suckers!" Cameron shouted as the Guardians began swinging at the departed, unaffected by the overhead energy drain. Shredding departed as they went, two Guardians were closing in on Seth and Brit.

Liam called to them, "The Caller Coin. Do you have it?"

"Yes," Seth called back.

"Protect you and Brit. Hold it in your hand. They answer the commands of the one closest to them who holds a coin. Cameron doesn't expect you to have one."

Seth pulled out the Coin and held it tight in his hand. "What about you?" Seth yelled as the third Guardian headed Liam's way.

"I'm good," Liam called back, picking up an old branch that broke in two when he swung it at the approaching beast.

Marie LeClaire

The ghosts repeated their downward assault, hundreds of them. Their continued energy drain was starting to affect the soldiers who were moving slower now with less coordination. One was already down on his knees as the ghosts continued to pound him.

Just as things were looking bleak for the Legion's squad, more Guardians appeared, along with six Legion officers armed with shredding weapons.

Malik took one look around and shouted, "Go! Now!"

Instantly his officers and Guardians went on the attack. They quickly identified the correct maneuvers of an upward over-the-head swing and the departed started falling, unrecognizable, into misty puddles.

The melee continued. The ghosts kept coming. Legions kept swinging.

"Stop! Stop!" Seth shouted repeatedly at the Guardians approaching him. Apparently, the Coin only commanded one Guardian at a time. He was holding the two at bay by continually shouting stop at the one nearest to them as he and Brit backed away. When the front Guardian stopped, the one behind moved forward, requiring another command. Although effective, it was only a short-term solution and one of them would soon hopscotch close enough to grab them.

Liam backed away from his attacker, looked around for weapon, then fell backward. He was sprawled out for the Guardian's final blow, when he felt something in his hand. It was the disappearing dagger.

"You're kidding?" he said to it, then grasped it tightly. The Guardian was standing over him with raised sword when Liam noticed the beast was standing on his coat. He rolled quickly between the beast's legs, jerking his coat quickly from underneath it's feet. The Guardian went down, giving Liam time to set up an attack. He knew the dagger wouldn't kill it, but it might slow it down.

As Seth's attacker closed in, in a panic, Seth shouted, "Stop him!" and pointed to the Guardian furthest away. To Seth's shock, the one commanded, instantly turned and decapitated the rear Guardian.

Catching on quickly, he shouted, "Protect us." The Guardian turned and took up a defensive position in front of Seth and Brit.

Looking around quickly, Seth asked, "Where's Simeon?"

"He joined the assault. I lost track of him," Sarah replied.

They looked around the cemetery. Ghosts were being slaughtered at a crazy rate.

Liam squared off against the Guardian again, dagger in hand. They were circling each other when a flash of light illuminated the scene. Four individuals in maroon robes appeared accompanied by one Guardian.

"It's the Consortium," Liam yelled.

Each Consortium counselor took out a small hand gun and began firing at the Guardians. Once hit, a Guardian would become covered in white dust, momentarily freeze, then collapse to the ground.

After seeing four Guardians go down easily, Malik assessed it would be a losing battle. "Fall back," he yelled. The remaining Guardians vanished through portals taking with them all Legion personnel and the fallen Guardians.

The sudden quiet of the cemetery was striking. The Consortium counselors remained where they were, surveying the scene. Liam was on the ground again, just about to be dispatched when his attacker disappeared. Seth and Brit were holding their breath, Seth's grip so tight on the Caller Coin that his hand would be sore for a week.

Piles and puddles of vapor were thick across the ground. The departed who were uninjured were starting to materialize, one by one. Puss was hovering above the tombstones, taking stock, his face somber.

One Guardian remained, dressed in the maroon robes of the Consortium.

Puss floated slowly over the scene while others remained silent. He floated over to Fay, a Guardian at her side.

"Is the Consortium making its own Guardians these days, Madam Chairman?" he asked.

"Don't be ludicrous, Sour Puss. We have been working on ways to turn them around, to break their allegiance to the Legion."

"And the side arms?" Liam asked as he dusted himself off.

"An exploding pellet of lime dust. It kills them, if you can say that about things that are already dead."

"Interesting. Not to seem ungrateful but what are you doing here?"

"We suspected there might be some trouble when we were alerted that the gate was opened," Fay replied.

Thanks for the assist. We'll be getting on our way," Liam nodded to Seth and Brit. Simeon, Sarah and James had gathered at their side. James was being supported by Simeon, his arm was a vapory mess.

"Seriously, Liam? You don't think you're going to just walk out of here with an Opener, do you?"

"I think he is," said Seth, holding up his Caller Coin. "Unless you're going to kill me."

The Mistaken Haunting of Seth Harrison

Fay's back straightened. "The Consortium does not resort to barbarism. We simply would like to talk to you."

"And I simply would *not* like that." Seth stared her down.

"Young man, you have no idea what you have gotten yourself into. You will need our support going forward."

"I don't know about that. It seems like the Dearly Departed have my back." Simeon, Sarah and James all started posturing and making gestures of power and agreement.

"You won't win this one, Fay," Liam said. "Let it go for another day." He walked over to join the others.

"Very well, Liam. But you and I are not finished. We still have business to resolve." Fay hesitated a moment, "and maybe some information to share."

"Maybe. But not tonight." He addressed the others. "Let's go."

Liam, Seth and Brit walked slowly back to the car, exhausted. Simeon, Sarah and James floated behind.

Chapter 33

Seth jumped in the back seat as usual, followed by Simeon. James and Sarah found room in the trunk with their heads sticking up behind the back seat, and Liam and Brit took the front seats.

As soon as they left the parking lot, Seth let out a long exhale. "That was crazy!"

"Right?" Brit nodded.

"Liam, is that going to be the end of it?" Seth asked, although he was pretty sure he knew the answer.

"Far from it. But the good news is that both the Consortium and the Legion know you're not going to play their game. At least not the way they thought."

"I'm not playing it any way at all," Seth insisted.

Liam looked at Seth in the rear-view mirror. "Don't be so quick to burn bridges, at least with the Consortium. And don't expect that the Legion is going to walk away nicely. To them, control of the Links is money, pure and simple."

"So, what should we do?" Brit almost pleaded.

"Things will be calm for the time being. Right now, I'll drop Sarah and James back off in Salem, then we can head home."

"Can't they come home with us?"

Marie LeClaire

Liam looked in the mirror to see James and Sarah slowly shaking their heads. "They need their touchstones."

James and Sarah nodded. Then Sarah started miming, her fingers touching in a triangle using her hands and forearms pointing skyward and then making a wavy motion with her hands.

"Water," Brit called out.

Sarah nodded emphatically, then made the triangle again and water going underneath.

"Bridgewater," Seth answered.

"You want me to drop you at Bridgewater and you'll use the link?"

They nodded.

"Right. Definitely faster for you, and much shorter for us. Thanks," Liam agreed.

"Liam, what did the Chairperson mean that you still had business?" Seth was somewhere between curious and suspicious.

"It's complicated. I sometimes do work for them. I told you that. She wants to know what I know about the Link at Fall River and probably what I know about you. In exchange she'll give me information about my father."

"What?" Brit was shocked. "That's terrible."

"Maybe. But that's the game."

"Are you going to give me up?" Seth asked.

"Of course not. But I will share enough information to get what I want. Finding my father has always been my first priority. As far as I'm concerned you and Brit are free agents. Do what you want."

"Can I still stay with you?" Seth almost whispered the question.

"Of course. I mean that. You can stay with me for as long as you like. Nothing changes."

The Mistaken Haunting of Seth Harrison

"Except everything," Brit pointed out.

"Yeah," Seth agreed as he slumped down in the seat.

Liam tried to ease the tension. "You're in possession of a Caller Coin. That gives you a certain amount of protection from the Legion. You are the only one that can open and close Links, so no one will kill you."

"Great." Seth slumped a little lower.

"I just mean you're in a good position right now. I'll talk to Fay tomorrow and get a feel for what they want out of this. In the meantime, let's all recover and figure out how to go forward."

Liam pulled the car over to the roadside a short distance from the Bridgewater prison and opened a window for James and Sarah to float out of.

Brit leaned over the seat. "Will we see you tomorrow?"

Sarah nodded.

"Okay. Good night." She waved to them as the vaped out of the car.

Liam pulled back into traffic and they headed home.

Chapter 35

Liam was sliding his computer into a valise along with some transcripts Fay had given him. Three weeks had passed without incident and Liam felt Seth and Brit would be okay for the time being.

"How long will you be gone?" Seth asked.

"Depends on what I find in London. I have Consortium business as well as a lead on my father."

"What if something happens while you're gone?" Brit's brows furrowed.

"You'll both be fine. Besides, Fay has given you one of the converted Guardians. All you have to do is call it."

"I don't really like having one. First of all, it feels wrong to own it. And I definitely don't like ordering it around."

"By the way," Brit asked, looking around. "Where is that thing when we don't see it?".

"I have no idea. The Guardian break room?" Liam balanced his valise on the suitcase that was packed and waiting by the door. "Only call it if you need it. Otherwise, go about your day, do your thing."

"Right." Seth agreed.

"And classes start in two weeks. No parties at the house. Mildred will be here to keep an eye on things. I can't prove it, but I think she has something going on with the Consortium."

Seth was enrolled in the local community college. Brit was starting her Senior year in High School.

Just then, Mildred strolled through her door.

Meeeeooooorrrwww mew mew.

"I'll miss you too, Mildred." Brit scooped her up into a hug. Mildred purred with pleasure.

They walked with Liam out to meet the Consortium car that had arrived to take him to the airport. Liam shook hands with Seth and then was ambushed by Brit with a bear hug that Seth quickly joined in on.

They waved as the car drove away. Simeon, James and Sarah watched and waved from behind a hedge. Mildred sat on the front stoop, feigning disinterest.

Marie LeClaire

Other books by Marie LeClaire
Available on Amazon.com, Barnes and Noble, Rakuten: Kobo and other reading platforms.

The Last Yard Sale
Four enchanted yard sale treasures show a lonely shop owner the way back to love.

When Marybeth stumbles upon an extraordinary yard sale, she has no idea how much her life is about to change.

Psychic visions explode in her mind as she touches each of four items for sale. Reluctantly, she takes them home. One by one, the objects and the visions reveal family secrets that force her to re-examine who she is. With a little heart and some dry humor, she forges ahead.

Meanwhile Josh Anderson, a lonely writer, breaks free from his self-imposed isolation to undertake a heartbreaking task of his own.

The Mistaken Haunting of Seth Harrison

When their business relationship turns romantic, they both struggle with old fears. Will she be able to let go of the past and open herself up to love again? Will he?

A Soldier's Last Mission (Sequel to The Last Yard Sale)

A mysterious yard sale sends a Vietnam vet on a mission to save the life of an Afghanistan soldier.

When Marybeth, a secondhand shop owner, acquires an old army helmet and some love letters at a mysterious yard sale, she doesn't know where to start. Visions of a young soldier's departure for war are seared into her brain. The soldier's plea to save my son's life swirl in her head. At the same time Marybeth's boyfriend, Josh, gets a cryptic message from his deceased mother, and drives the four hours from Connecticut to Pennsylvania to check in on her. Together they begin to unravel the mystery set in motion by the yard sale. When they enlist the help of her father Sean, a Vietnam vet, they find themselves way out of their league.

When Sean realizes the helmet is his, swapped with another soldier in combat forty years ago, he's gripped with guilt. The other soldier had not survived the battle. He also hears the soldier's plea, save my son's life and immediately calls in reinforcements, his VA buddies. The whole crew embarks on a mission to save a recently retired soldier from himself. But it won't be easy. First, they have to find him.

One Thousand Buddhas: But Who's Counting

Four strangers.
A young executive about to get married
A young woman seeking adventure
A man running away from his bad boy past
A widower looking for meaning

Four missions to save the Buddhas.
A twenty-three-year-old in Japan
A thirteen-year-old in Chicago
A newborn boy in Guam
A baby girl in New York City

Buddhist prophecy says that when one thousand Buddhas have been born, humanity will evolve into a new level of understanding, but only if they survive.

Nathan stumbles upon a monk in a cave who sends him on a quest to find an unknown thirteen-year-old boy in Chicago. Will he find him? If he does, will he be able to keep him safe?

Three other people have similar missions. At least one must be successful.

***

Four strangers are recruited by a mysterious monk in a cave in the Himalayas to find the last four Buddhas and keep them safe. Nathan must find a thirteen-year-old boy in in Chicago. Sarah- a baby girl in Guam. Akio - a young woman in Okinawa. And Leo must locate at newborn baby boy in New York City. If they fail? The end of the human race. Their adversary is mankind itself. And time is running out.

The Old Wool Factory

(This book has an accompanying crochet pattern purchased separately at ColourSpun.com)

When Gabby is let in on the family secret, she soon learns that what she thinks becomes real and intention is everything.

Gabby was living with her boyfriend, Dylan, in Albany, New York, until her mother died. Called upon to care for the family matriarch, she arrives in Branford, an hour and a half south of Buffalo, with only one goal – to leave. But family secrets abound and a legacy appears that she finds hard to believe. Nanna thinks there's magic in the crochet stitches she uses. Gabby thinks she's crazy.

Marie LeClaire

Jason Khern is an entrepreneur with an environmental conscience. He has his eye on an old wool factory upstate for his new business venture.

Is it Nanna's meddling that brings them together or is it magic?

About the Author

Marie LeClaire has spent the past thirty years as a mental health counselor encouraging others to look beyond our sometimes-limited perspective and see a bigger picture of what influences our lives and guides our behavior. She has been writing novels and short stories for the past five years. She still does a little counseling part time, but her love now is purely fiction - sort of. After all, art imitates life, doesn't it? After wandering around much of her adult life, she currently calls Worcester, MA home.

Made in the USA
Coppell, TX
05 December 2023